MW01142754

Advance praise for *Murder Manhattan Style*

In this collection, Warren Bull takes his readers across the American landscape with stories of justice and injustice, truth and speculation, and humor and noir. The Manhattan in the title sometimes refers to the suave part of New York and sometimes to its prairie twin in Kansas. The stories are equally diverse. Bull writes tales of children outwitting their elders in the name of what's right in turbulent Bleeding Kansas; of card sharks, clever dames and tough guys out on the town in the flush days of post-World War II; of an anguished husband and another furious father thwarted while seeking revenge; and a crime writer who really can't handle rejection. Bull proposes intriguing questions—What if the ghost of Hamlet's father wasn't an apparition after all?—and moral ones—At what point is personal danger more tolerable than the loss of human dignity? Warren Bull is a thoughtful, gifted writer who blends history, language, pathos and a fine wit to tell terrific stories.

> –Ramona DeFelice Long, independent editor and author

Witty, charming and clever, Warren Bull's stories capture perfectly the plains of Manhattan, Kansas; the mean streets of Manhattan, New York; and everything in between. His characters sparkle with humor and smarts.

> –Lisa Harkrader, author of *Nocturne*, a YA fantasy, and
> winner of the William Allen White Award
> for *Airball: My Life in Briefs*

Warren Bull is a short story master, and this collection shows him at his best with quick stories told in crisp, clear prose. There's variety, drama, history, humor, pathos, compassion and even Shakespeare here, along with surprising and satisfying endings to every story.

> –Nancy Pickard, *New York Times* Bestselling Author

Murder Manhattan Style by Warren Bull is a collage of well-written stories as different as their settings, ranging from the Manhattan in Kansas to the town of the same name in New York, with whistle stops along the way. Characters are as diverse as a young brother and sister encountering crime and prejudice in 1850's Middle America, tough-talking gumshoes of the 1930's and '40's Big Apple, to some who practice crime in the present day. Even a delightful homage visit with guys and dolls in Damon Runyon mode, those lovable characters who begin each day with the racing form and end it with whatever scheme looks profitable.

Wherever and whenever these well-drawn characters play out their stories, there's more to savor than what they do and say. Underlying each engaging tale is a glimpse of what's going on in their minds and how they mentally process what's going on around them. It takes a practicing psychologist to relate that element so sharply, and, fortunately for readers of these stories, that's precisely what Warren Bull happens to be when he's not writing fiction.

Highly recommended morsels for when you want to spice up your reading diet with variety.

–Earl Staggs, Derringer Award winner
and author of *Memory of a Murder*

MURDER

Manhattan Style

MURDER

Manhattan Style

Warren Bull

Ninth Month Publishing Co.
Sedona, Arizona

Murder Manhattan Style
Copyright 2010 by Warren Bull
180 Pages
First Edition
ISBN 13: 978-0-9822271-3-8
ISBN 10: 0-9822271-3-2

Published by
Ninth Month Publishing Co.
365 Northview Road
Sedona, AZ 86336

Manufactured in the United States; printed by Wordpro Press, Ithaca, NY

Credits:
Cover Art by Ginnie E.L. Fenton (Copyright 2010)

"A Detective's Romance," Copyright 2010 by Warren Bull
"A Lady of Quality," previously published in *DowngoSun* September 2006.
Copyright 2006 by Warren Bull
"Beecher's Bibles," previously appeared in *Manhattan Mysteries,* KS Pub-
lishing, Inc. (2004). Copyright 2004 by Warren Bull
"Butterfly Milkweed," previously appeared in *Crimeandsuspense.com* May
2006. Copyright 2006 by Warren Bull
"Funeral Games," previously appeared in *The Back Alley,* November 2007.
Copyright 2007 by Warren Bull
"Java Judy," Copyright 2010 by Warren Bull
"Kansas Justice," Copyright 2010 by Warren Bull
"Locard's Principle," previously appeared in *Great Mystery and Suspense
Magazine* Fall and Winter 2006. Copyright 2006 by Warren Bull
"Murder at the GMMC," previously appeared in *Mysterical-E* Spring 2007.
Copyright 2007 by Warren Bull
"One Sweet Scam," previously appeared in *Sniplits.com* April 2008 and is

I would like to thank my wife, Judy; my parents, Dorris and Ivan; my siblings, Dennis, Peggy and Tina; and my friends for their unwavering support. I would like to thank the many people who help the Great Manhattan Mystery Conclave work its magic. I'd also like to thank members of Westport Writers' Workshop, StorySuccess and Border Crimes and Barnes & Noble critique groups who greatly improved my efforts. This book is dedicated to the memory of Doreen Shanteau, treasurer, board member and enthusiastic supporter of the Great Manhattan Mystery Conclave; and Robert L. Iles, author, mentor and friend.

The Great Manhattan Mystery Conclave

Ever since attending the first Great Manhattan Mystery Conclave in October 2004, the voices in my head have been getting louder and more demanding. I'm a psychologist in my day job so I know that can be a problem. On the other hand, as a writer I've learned that allowing the voices to tell their stories in words on paper gives them satisfaction. It gives me a sense of relief.

Although I signed up late and arrived at the last moment for the first conference and had only one mystery publication to my name, I felt accepted and supported in my efforts as an author. Over the course of five conferences, I met first-rate mystery authors and editors whose work I truly admired (and still do) and who were amazingly approachable and helpful, including in no particular order: Nancy Pickard, Carolyn Hart, Susan McBride, Susan Albert Whiting, Chris Roerden, Rob Walker, Mike Hays, Lisa Harkrader, Mark Bouden, Joel Goldman, Sally Goldenbaum, JoAnn Carl, Radine Trees Nehring, Diane Mott Davidson and Will Thomas.

The organizers, including Marolyn Caldwell, Bruce Gbur, Robin Higham, Bob Claar, Karen Ingram, Kim Dillon, Doreen Shanteau, Stormy Lee Kennedy, Dennis Toll, Don Hochman and Felisa Osburn, put in many hours of work and created a friendly small-town atmosphere that has carried over to all five conclaves. Cheryl Collins, Mike Finnegan, Jim Shanteau, Al Riniker, Steve Osburn, William E. Kennedy III and others have contributed to the success of the conclave.

Contents

Beecher's Bibles

The Kansas Territory, Miller Farm, April 28, 1858

When the two riders appeared out of nowhere, I knew they came to kill my pa. I'd seen smoldering burned-out farmhouses. I'd heard women cry and pray in church because riders had appeared during the night and called their husbands out to answer the question, "Are you for or against slavery?" The wrong answer or even a slow answer meant that the men were taken away and never seen again.

My pa was against slavery. When anybody asked, he made no bones about it. He didn't preach about it. He didn't ride with the Jayhawkers. According to my pa, violence was just as wrong when we did it as when they did it. That didn't matter to these men. These men and others like them had turned the territory into "Bleeding Kansas."

I didn't recognize the riders. One was tall, thin and clean-shaven. The other was stout and bearded. They rode as quietly as ghosts, careful to blend in with the lay of the land. They stopped outside our farmhouse and looked down at me like hawks looking at a prairie dog. I knew I didn't look like much, being just twelve and small enough to pass for ten. They looked tough enough to take on a hundredfold of me.

"We'd like to speak with your father," said the tall one.

1

I swallowed and answered, "He's not here right now." I was glad to be speaking the truth. I think the man would have known if I lied. Earlier this morning, a man on a lathered bay mare rushed to the house to tell my pa something. They spoke briefly. Then my pa saddled his long-legged roan and insisted that the man switch his tack to our gray stallion that could run all day. They put the bay in the barn, and after a few words with my stepmother, Sarah, they left.

"When will he be back?" the shorter man asked.

"He didn't say," I answered.

As if there wasn't already enough trouble, my stepsister, Amy, came running up just then. Her dress was wet and dirty below the knees. Her hair was full of briars. I could tell that she'd been playing by Wildcat Creek. She was not supposed to, but I knew this wasn't the time to quarrel. She wouldn't listen, anyway. Even though she was a year younger than me, she was my height. She could run faster, fight harder and shoot straighter than I could. Earlier that morning we each took four shots with a Sharps rifle at a target twenty-five paces away. Amy fired faster than I did and she hit with all her shots. I missed twice.

"Are you two here alone?" asked the tall man.

"Pa left," said Amy. "Then a neighbor came by to fetch Ma. He said his wife was feeling poorly."

The stout man chuckled, but he didn't sound friendly. "Two children left alone in these troubled times?"

The tall man answered, "Why not? It would be a poor excuse for a man who would bother a woman or a child."

"My name is Joshua," I said, belatedly remembering my manners. No matter who these men were, I had been taught to be polite. "This is my stepsister, Amy. I'm sorry that my pa and my stepmother are away. If you'd care to tell us who you are, we'll

2

be certain to tell Pa that you stopped by."

"You can call me Mr. Anders," said the tall man. "You can call him Mr. Bleak. Maybe we'll keep you company until your pa comes back."

"Would you like us to water and feed your horses and turn them into the corral?" asked Amy.

"Thank you, Amy," said Anders, "but we're used to caring for our own animals. I think we'll put them in the barn to get them out of the sun."

Amy gave me a sharp look. She might not have been the girl I would have chosen for a sister, but nobody ever said she was stupid. If the horses were left in the corral, my pa could tell long before he came to the house that strangers were here. With the horses in the barn, he would have no way of knowing. Anders and Bleak led their horses toward the barn, and we followed. Amy turned her back to the men and put her right hand over her heart with her fingers together pointing down. She moved her hand up and down from her wrist.

Silently I thanked my pa for teaching us Indian sign language. I saw the men were not looking at me. I clasped my hands together over the chest like two men shaking hands. Then, using my right hand, I pressed my index finger against my thumb and flicked the finger forward. Amy signed, "Trouble." I signed, "Agree" and "Talk."

Amy darted ahead of the men into the barn. She pulled a bucket from a peg on the wall.

"We'll get water," she said.

We walked toward the well, with Amy carrying the bucket. I looked back. The men stopped outside the barn. The tall man waved at me and I waved back.

"They're here after Pa," said Amy.

3

"I think so, too."

"We have to do something," said Amy.

"But what?"

"When we get to the well, I'll run," said Amy. "I'm fast."

"Not as fast as a man on horseback."

"Then we'll both run. They'll chase you, and I can make it to the hideout."

I answered, "If you do, you'll be stuck there. If you leave, they'll see you. You can't warn Pa from there."

We reached the well, and, to my relief, Amy did not run. We lowered the bucket. I felt like my stomach was sinking with it. My legs felt wobbly.

Amy said, "From here I can get into the house and load a rifle before they catch me."

"Then you'll have one rifle against two. If you shoot one man, the other will shoot you. That won't help Pa."

We hauled up the bucket.

"We can pretend we think the men are Pa's friends," I said. "We can invite them into the house."

"Why?"

"Because if they want to come in, we can't stop them," I answered.

We filled the bucket with water.

"Let's pretend they're Pa's friends," I said. "They might relax a little. We'll get a chance to do something later. If we try and fail now, they could tie us up and gag us. Then we couldn't help Pa. We'll get only one chance."

Amy took one side of the bucket's handle, and I took the other. We lifted it and slowly headed back.

"What's your plan?" asked Amy.

"I don't have one," I answered. "We have to wait for a

4

good chance. We have to recognize it and act."

"If Pa comes home before we can act," said Amy, "I'll jump them and scratch their eyes out."

"If that times comes," I said, "you jump the one closest to you and I'll use my pocketknife on the other one."

I knew that, if that time came, Amy and I would be in trouble and Pa wouldn't have a prayer. Amy and I together couldn't take either man alone on his worst day. One on one, we had no chance at all. But we had to try. We carried the bucket into the barn and poured the water into a trough.

When Anders entered, he spotted the bay. He studied it.

"That's one fine mare," said Anders.

"She's not ours," Amy said. "I don't know who she belongs to."

It appeared to me that Anders and Bleak knew.

Bleak removed the tack from his horse and tossed it on the gate to the stall. Then he shifted from foot to foot as he waited for Anders. Anders carefully checked his horse over. He looked at its knees, looked in its mouth and raised each hoof in turn. He rubbed the animal down. Before leaving the stall, he made sure it had food and water. I noticed that each man carried a rifle and wore a Bowie knife at his waist.

We invited the men into our house. Bleak went straight to the fireplace and snatched a biscuit out of the Dutch oven on the hearth. He ate it right there, dropping crumbs on his beard and on the floor as he leaned his rifle against the wall. Anders took off his hat and looked over the room.

I said, "Please, if you're hungry, we have plenty of food."

"I could fix you a plate," offered Amy.

"Much obliged," answered Anders. "I could eat a biscuit if you have enough to go around."

"Of course we do," answered Amy. "Please take a seat." She got out a plate, a knife and a jar of apple butter. Bleak stuffed his mouth full like a ravenous wolf. Amy took the last biscuit out of the Dutch oven. Anders set his rifle within easy reach and sat down at the table.

"What's this?" asked Bleak, wiping his mouth with his sleeve and scattering crumbs. He reached above the fireplace and pulled a rifle off its pegs. "Is this one of them new Sharps?"

"Yes, sir," answered Amy.

"That's a breech-loading percussion rifle," said Anders. "I've never seen one before but I've heard about them."

Months ago, when Pa brought two Sharps rifles home, he explained that they were only to be used in self-defense. My stepmother had asked, "Are these what they call 'Beecher Bibles'?"

Pa had smiled. "Yes, Reverend Henry Ward Beecher argues that we must be ready to defend ourselves. Some of the rifles were smuggled in using boxes labeled 'Church Supplies.' I suppose it doesn't hurt that Mr. Sharps's first name is Christian."

We had all laughed.

"Now," my pa had said, "listen to the commandments: Always act as if these rifles are loaded. Never point them at a person unless you mean to shoot that person. Never cock the hammer and pull the trigger unless there's a cap on the cone where the hammer lands. Otherwise, the cone can crack. Always clean the rifle thoroughly after ten shots at most. Powder is forced backward into the works with each shot. It can jam the works. Powder left in the muzzle makes shooting inaccurate."

Bleak burped explosively, which brought my attention back to the present.

"How does it work?" asked Bleak.

Beecher's Bibles

Anders took the rifle. "There should be a catch. Here it is." He pushed the trigger guard all the way forward. The breech-block inside the Sharps dropped down, leaving the path to the chamber free.

Bleak grabbed the rifle. "Let me see." He worked the lever back and forth rapidly. "It's like a bucket dropping into a well."

Anders walked over to the mantel and looked at a box of cartridges and the open bag of caps.

"The cartridge must go into the breech," said Anders, "not down the muzzle."

"Yes, sir," I said. "You push the cartridge into the chamber with the ball forward. Then you move the lever back."

Amy rolled her eyes but kept quiet. Didn't she see that Anders would have figured that out on his own? We had to pretend to cooperate.

"What do you do then?" asked Anders, picking up a cap.

Amy said, "You half cock the hammer and fit a cap over the cone where the hammer strikes. You don't want to fully cock the hammer until you're ready to fire."

"You just aim and fire once the hammer is fully cocked?" asked Anders. "And for the second shot you just repeat the steps?"

"You have to remove the old cap and put a new one on the cone each time," said Amy. Smart girl. Anders would have known that after he fired the weapon one time.

I remembered that, after my pa was sure we could take care of the rifle, he had insisted that Amy, her mother and I learn how to shoot. Sarah didn't like to fire the rifle but she quickly became a steady shooter. Amy, of course, took to it like a duck to water. I had the most problems. We could not figure out why I shot so

7

poorly. Then Amy noticed that, just before I fired, I closed my eyes.

"You can't hit what you don't see," my pa had said. "Lots of people close their eyes because of the flash and the noise. You'll have to practice staying calm and shooting slowly."

I had gotten better with practice, but I never caught up with Amy or her mother.

Anders whistled and said, "In the time it takes to load and fire a muzzleloader once, even a woman or a child could fire this rifle two or three times."

Bleak quickly went through the loading process without a cap or a cartridge and pulled the trigger. The hammer snapped home. He did it twice more.

Amy said, "That was pretty fast, but I can do it faster."

Bleak shoved the lever forward, yanked it back, cocked the hammer and jerked the trigger. Snap. He did it over and over, faster and faster. Snap followed snap followed snap.

"That's enough," said Anders. He walked over to the second Sharps, which was leaning against the wall. Amy and I had used that one to practice with earlier that morning. We had argued about whose turn it was to clean the rifle and neither of us had cleaned it. Of course we would before my father got home. Anders picked up the rifle and checked the works. "I want to shoot with this."

I picked up two boxes of cartridges and a bag of caps. I took them to him.

"Can I come along?" I asked.

I showed him the stump Amy and I used for target practice.

Anders shaved the bark away making a circle about the size of his fist. He paced off thirty paces and put five shots close enough together that a silver dollar could cover all five. Then he stepped back another ten paces and shot again five times. All shots were inside the circle.

"I wish I could shoot like that," I said.

"Take the rifle and sight in on the stump," said Anders. "Leave the hammer down and just point at the stump." Anders stepped behind me and bent over. "You have it sighted well. You're holding it steady. Now load the rifle."

I did. I had a loaded weapon and Anders didn't. But he was too close. I couldn't swing the barrel around fast enough. Besides, Amy was still in the farmhouse with Bleak.

"You need to relax," said Anders. "Breathe deep, point the rifle and squeeze the trigger gently. Don't worry about aiming. Just point and squeeze."

The gun went off. "Sometimes I close my eyes," I admitted.

"Lots of men do," said Anders. "You'd be surprised how many. Don't guess when the rifle will fire. Don't tug at the trigger. Don't try too hard to aim. Just load, point and squeeze."

I took seven more shots and handed the rifle back to Anders.

"Good job," said Anders. "You seem a lot more relaxed than when you first took the rifle. Let's check your shots."

I was so scared that I thought my knees would buckle as we walked toward the stump. With my heart racing, I pointed to the cluster of shots Amy had made that morning. Luckily, a few shots of mine were not far away.

"Good shooting," said Anders. "Let's head back."

When we got back to the farmhouse, we found Bleak gulping down the last of my stepmother's apple pie.

"It's getting late," said Bleak. "They should be returning soon. We could tie the children to the corral and use them for bait."

Amy glared at him. I balled my hands into fists.

"I don't make war on children," answered Anders. "We'll lock them in the storm cellar."

"Pa will expect us to come running out as soon as we see him," said Amy. "He'll be suspicious if we aren't around."

"He'll be worried," said Anders. "I can't let you give him a warning."

Amy feinted to her left and swung to her right. Anders took a half step toward her, cutting off her escape.

I ran at Bleak, my arms flailing. He backhanded me in the face, rattling my teeth. Then Bleak tossed me onto his shoulder like I was a sack of corn. I kicked and punched. It was like assaulting a buffalo barehanded. Bleak smelled of sweat, whiskey and smoke.

I saw Amy twist and dodge constantly. Anders moved only when he could force her closer to a corner of the room where she could not escape. In short order Anders snared her wrist and then had his hands on both arms.

We shouted and squirmed, but Anders and Bleak forced us into the cellar under the house. We heard something heavy scrape across the floor and settle over the cellar door.

"Yell!" I demanded, hammering on the underside of the door.

"Why?" asked Amy. "Oh." She shouted and banged on the door. After a few moments she put her finger to her lips. We listened intently. I could hear Amy breathing heavily but no sound came through the floor.

"Did Bleak come down here and look around?" I asked Amy.

"No," she said. "He played with the rifle and ate the whole

time. Some of our hogs have better table manners. Let's get out of here."

We moved the empty barrels that my pa had put in front of the hidden door and looked out through the peephole. We snuck into the house and looked around. Anders and Bleak left their muzzle-loading rifles in the house. They took our rifles, boxes of cartridges and the bag of caps.

"They're probably hidden in spots they can shoot from," said Amy. "We don't know where. We can't let them see us."

"Maybe," I said, "if we make a big circle and move quietly...."

Then we stopped. We could hear Pa calling us and he was close.

"Josh, Amy, come meet Mr. Brown."

We ran outside, shouting warnings. Time seemed to slow down. Wild flowers gleamed brightly. I could smell the horses and hear their hoofbeats. Bleak rose languidly from the ground and slowly lifted the rifle into position to shoot. Anders rose without haste from a spot to the left of Bleak. They had Pa and Mr. Brown in their sights. We kept shouting and running but we could not move fast enough to help. Bleak and Anders ignored us.

Bleak pulled the trigger. The Sharps flashed backwards into his face. Bleak screamed. Time resumed its normal speed.

Anders fired. Pa kicked the roan into a run toward us. Mr. Brown kept our gray stallion at a walk. He acted like this sort of thing happened all the time. Anders looked down at the Sharps. Mr. Brown pulled a pistol from his holster and pointed it at Anders.

Pa pulled the roan to a stop. "Are you hurt?"

I looked at Amy and she looked at me. "We're fine," I said.

"I'll get a wet cloth for Mr. Bleak," said Amy. When she returned, Mr. Brown had Anders and Bleak against the wall of the house. Pa was asking me questions faster than I could answer. Amy carried the wet cloth to Bleak. As she reached up toward his burned face, Bleak grabbed her. He put one arm around her neck. With his other hand, he pulled his Bowie knife.

"Let me go or I'll cut her," said Bleak. Before I was aware of what I was doing, I ran at him and dived. I bounced off his leg. Bleak kicked at me and missed. Amy ducked her head. She bit his arm as hard as she could. Bleak screamed again. Anders smashed his fist into Bleak's face. Bleak dropped the knife and let go of Amy. He fell to the ground and whimpered.

Amy ran to our pa. Anders picked up Bleak's Bowie knife and threw it. It struck a fencepost with a thump, burying three inches of the blade into the wood. Anders then pulled out his own knife and threw it. It stuck in the same fencepost just above Bleak's. Anders looked down at Bleak.

"I don't make war on children," said Anders.

Mr. Brown tied Anders and Bleak to a long rope. He looped one end of the rope over his saddle horn, and then he mounted the bay.

"I'm taking these men to Fort Riley," said Mr. Brown.

"I'll bring the horses along tomorrow," said our pa. "I'll testify at their trial. Maybe the jury will take notice that Mr. Anders protected Amy."

Mr. Brown gave Pa an odd look. He touched his finger to his hat in a salute and started off with Bleak and Anders walking in front.

"All right, you two," said Pa. "Tell me how that happened."

"They seemed to come out of the ground," I said. "I didn't

12

see them coming. I'm sorry."

"Lawmen in Kansas have been looking for those men for months," said Pa. "They could sneak up on their own shadows. That's not what I want to know."

"I had no idea Mr. Bleak could see," said Amy. "I'm sorry he fooled me like that."

"I didn't know he could see, either, honey," said Pa. "You have a kind heart. You meant to help a man who had been your enemy. You have nothing to be sorry about. That's not what I meant, either. I want to know how two children outsmarted those outlaws."

We told him how. As usual, Amy went first.

"I got Mr. Bleak to dry-fire the Sharps so many times that the cone cracked. So when he fired the loaded rifle, powder blew back into his face."

I explained, "I got Mr. Anders to fire the other Sharps so many times without cleaning it that the muzzle filled with powder and the rifle lost accuracy. I'm surprised it fired at all."

Amy added, "Joshua charged Mr. Bleak so I could bite him and Mr. Anders could punch him."

I said, looking at Amy, "You could have run to Manhattan when the men first arrived. They didn't know you were here, but you didn't want to leave me alone with strangers."

"I didn't want them to hurt my brother," said Amy.

"I didn't want Mr. Bleak to hurt my sister," I answered.

Our pa blinked away tears. "I got dust in my eyes," he said. He swallowed.

"I still don't understand," said Amy. "How could Mr. Bleak see after the powder blew back into his eyes?"

"I don't know," said our pa.

"I do," I said. They looked at me. "Mr. Anders practiced

with a rifle so he knew what to expect. Mr. Bleak had never fired that kind of rifle before he tried to shoot you with it."

Pa said, "It's more likely that they wanted to kill John Brown. After the city of Lawrence was sacked and an abolitionist died, Mr. Brown and his sons killed five pro-slavery men. Now, the Border Ruffians want revenge on him." He shook his head. "Violence begets more violence."

"I'm glad they didn't want to shoot you," I said. "Anyway, Mr. Bleak wasn't sure how much his weapon would kick. He didn't know exactly when it would fire." I smiled. "So when he pulled the trigger, he closed his eyes."

Author's note: This was a first in several ways. It's the first children's story I wrote. It won the first writing award I received. It was one of the winners of the Great Manhattan Mystery Conclave's short story contest. It's the first story about a family I keep coming back to. Stories about other family members follow.

One peculiar thing about writing this story that I remember is that it took about as long to write the first sentence correctly as it took to write the rest of the story. I knew what I wanted to say, but not how to say it. I didn't really ever get the first sentence right. I just ran out of ways to write it incorrectly. Each revision got closer and closer to what I wanted until the final version was the only one left.

Kansas Justice

City of Manhattan, Kansas Territory, October 16, 1859

When Joshua and I crested the hill overlooking Manhattan, we saw a mess of people in the streets shouting and arguing with each other. They looked like ants after the anthill has been kicked over. A knot of men dragged two struggling people down the street. Some kicked and pummeled the unfortunates while others tried to pull them free.

"What's going on?" I asked.

"Looks like a lynch mob," answered Joshua. "Let's see what we can do."

I hesitated, feeling a lump in my throat, but Joshua took off and I followed. As we got closer, I recognized our friends and neighbors. Father Stone, a Catholic priest recently arrived from Maine, was shouting at Abram Walker, a red-faced horse trader nearly as big as the animals he sold. Walker's son, Billy, tugged at his sleeve, trying to pull his father back, but it was like trying to move a mountain.

Stone intoned, "Vengeance is mine sayeth the Lord."

Walker answered, "'Twasn't the Lord's horses that got stole. Was mine."

A ragged cheer came from the crowd when Daniel Evans, one of the local rowdies, tossed a rope with a noose tied in one end over the limb of a cottonwood tree. A few men stood stiff and silent in disapproval. Others cheered and whistled while they passed bottles around. They joked and laughed. I could smell the cheap whiskey.

Len Haskin and Zachary Bailey dragged the two men toward the tree. I could see that the men were Indians. Dressed in foul-smelling filthy rags, they struggled with their captors to no avail. Evans snatched up another hangman's rope to throw.

I didn't know what to do. Seeing friends and neighbors act as part of a mob was the worst thing I had ever seen. I might be only twelve and just a girl, as the boys liked to point out, but I had seen things since I came to the Kansas Territory that would make a strong man go weak in the knees. I'd seen a stillborn infant, perfect with its tiny fingernails and eyelashes but born dead for reasons only God understood. I'd watched a man shake, go rigid and die after he tripped while plowing and fell upon a rattlesnake that struck him in the breast. I'd seen the smoky, charred remains of burned farmhouses. In church I'd heard the crying of women and children whose husbands and fathers had been called out from their homes at night, never to return. When nightriders asked the dreaded question, "Where do you stand on slavery?" the wrong answer or just a slow answer was fatal. Either answer might be wrong. Two men set on killing Pa came to our farm, but Joshua and I had survived even that. Now, I stood as if frozen, all thought chased from my mind by fear.

Joshua spoke a few words to Johann Smit, an old settler, borrowed the shotgun he carried and blasted both barrels into the air.

The crowd fell silent. Joshua handed the shotgun back, stepped forward and announced, "There's been enough killing without legal authority. There will be no lynching today."

I ran to his side, thinking that he had spoken well. Many in the assembly had lost friends or family members to Border Ruffians or Jayhawkers. A few of the roughnecks rode with one side or the other. They were reluctant to make the first move. Billy Walker moved to Joshua's side, and his scowling brother, Joseph, came to join him. Little Clemmie Carlson tottered over to us, carrying her rag doll to show me. I picked her up and rocked her back and forth as she giggled. I looked Haskins, Bailey and the Evans brothers in the eye. They turned their heads to look away. Back east, we would have been considered children and told to stay out of adult matters. Here on the frontier we had already earned a measure of respect.

Father Stone called out, "And a little child shall lead them. Are you so determined to commit murder that you will slash your way through your children to do so? Have you no shame at all?"

I held my breath as the mob remained silent for several heartbeats.

Finally Abram Walker spoke up.

"What are you doing, boy?"

Joshua said, "Preventing you, sir, from doing something you will regret later."

Walker spat back, "Stealing horses is a hanging offense." His voice shook with anger.

"'Tis and rightly so," I piped up. "Leave a man horseless on the plains and you likely condemn him to death."

"That's what these Indians did," said Walker. He crossed his arms and stared down at us.

Joshua shot me a glance that let me know I was not helping.

Joshua said, "If that's what a jury decides or what the soldiers determine, then they can be hung legally. I don't see any lawmen here."

People in the crowd muttered and argued among themselves.

"We got no jail to hold 'em," said Walker. "Who knows when the sheriff will return? I don't aim to take all day and march them off to Fort Riley." He looked at the crowd again, gauging the reaction of the people. "It was my horses they stole. I got an interest in this. I say we have enough men here to pick a judge and a jury. I believe we can trust in our neighbors to give fair and honest judgment. We can have our own court and give these heathens a proper trial right here. We even have a tree handy for when the verdict is handed down."

The men in the crowd who had been looking for excitement cheered. The steadier element murmured, but nobody objected. With few lawmen over the vast territory, frontier justice was often raw and final. Our only hope was that people had a sense of fairness.

"Do you reckon we can do better?" Joshua asked me.

"I don't think so. If we refuse, the Indians might get strung up anyway."

"Are you ready to take the responsibility of defending their lives?" Joshua asked me.

"I am if you are," I said.

"Let's agree to the rules to make it proper," said Walker in a loud voice. "We each get to nominate judge, bailiffs and jurors. If we are in accord, that man is accepted; if not, another nomination is made. Each side takes a turn until both are satisfied."

I looked at Joshua, who nodded.

"Done," I replied.

Walker frowned. I realized he was trying to ignore me, but I was determined I would not be ignored. He had few dealings with women and I suspicioned that, like a lot of men, he had little respect for women outside what he thought of as their place.

"Why don't you choose first?" I asked.

Walker jumped at the chance. After accepting my offer, he could not exclude me from the discussion.

"I choose Olaf Carlson for judge," said Walker.

The toughs and idlers laughed. Carlson was slow of speech and he sometimes stuttered. I thought Walker expected us to reject Carlson so he could then suggest a man whose thinking ran more along his own lines. Walker was known as an honest man, but one as hard as the flint abundant in the hills in this part of the prairie.

"Done," answered Joshua. We knew Carlson to be a fair man who took his responsibilities seriously. Walker looked surprised, but he could not take back his own choice. The rowdies laughed and joked like they were at a circus.

"For bailiffs I choose Len Haskin and Zachary Bailey," said Joshua.

"And the Evans brothers," I added. "With a crowd this size, we might need more than two."

Walker bit his lip. I thought he might object. We chose four men who hated Indians and who would have voted to hang them, regardless of the evidence. Now they could not be jurors. They were toughs with hair-trigger tempers who counted slights and casual remarks as terrible insults. They could control the drunks by their reputations alone. Walker risked offending them if he questioned their selection. Horse trader that he was, he managed to smile and congratulate the men on their appointments.

"You've named four men to my one," said Walker. "I reckon I ought to name four jurors."

Smit spoke up from the crowd. "You had first pick and chose the judge, Walker. That's advantage enough, especially for a horse trader. I say you alternate picking jurors, 'less you think them two young 'uns are too smart for you."

The crowd laughed. Walker's face reddened. In the end we alternated picks. Walker favored layabouts and idlers. We chose men who farmed their claims and took on work from others to make their way in the territory.

Walker wanted to jump right into the trial. I objected that we had not had time to talk with the accused and that we needed to plan our strategy. Carlson listened solemnly to each side and pondered for some moments. Then he spoke.

"Y-y-you have an hour." Then he added, "The jurors will not drink between now and the end of trial." The men Walker picked let out groans.

We moved away from the crowd. The bailiffs watched to make sure the Indians could not escape. Using Indian sign language, which Pa had insisted we learn, Joshua and I questioned the Indians.

The older Indian signed, "I, Red Hawk; son, Buffalo Tracker. We walk. Our people. West."

I signed, "Horses?"

Red Hawk signed, "No horses. Many Indians, no horses. Many white men, no horses."

He was certainly right about that. Many settlers had no horses. They walked everywhere or caught a ride on wagons headed in the direction they wanted to go. They bartered to get teams for plowing and harvest. Those who had horses used them only for work or travel. Our Pa had three horses and was considered rich. Walker always had at least a dozen horses of different breeds. He could rent you a team of plow horses, sell you a racer or supply you with a breeding mare.

Red Hawk continued, "Two boys ride horses. Kick, throw rocks. Grab."

I looked at Joshua. We knew that had to be Billy and Joseph Walker. None of the other youngsters had horses. Billy and Joseph would sneak away from their chores and ride around looking for a boy off by himself to torment and bedevil. Although they were big like their father, they preferred to gang up on a smaller boy and then ride off before adults caught them. Walker made use of a heavy leather strap on his sons when they were caught, but that only seemed to make them meaner and sneakier. Billy and Joseph lorded it over all the boys in the area because they had mustangs that had been caught and tamed. Some boys pretended to be their friends just to get an occasional ride.

Red Hawk signed, "Big man. Yell boys. Talk. Fight us. Drag us here. Drunk white men. Kick, beat. Hang soon."

Joshua signed, "Maybe not. We help. You stay."

Red Hawk frowned and nodded. He signed running and being shot.

I signed, "Big man?"

Buffalo Tracker pointed toward Walker.

We talked to Walker next.

Walker said, "You'll hear what my boys said in testimony pretty soon. They told me they caught the Indians trying to make off with my horses. They shut the horses in the barn and set out to take the thieves to the law. I admit I got hot under the collar. The sheriff was out of town. In a fit of anger, I persuaded some of the men to string them up. We shouldn't have done that, but I was not hanging them just because they were Indians. You know I trade with Indians. I don't hold with those who mistreat them just for being what God made them."

"I believe you, sir," said Joshua. "I know you to be an honest man. Thank you."

We retreated to plan our strategy.

"I believe Red Hawk and Buffalo Tracker more than Billy and Joseph," I said.

"So do I," answered Joshua. "Likely they were bothering the Indians when their father rode up and they seized upon a tall tale in hopes of escaping a beating. Mr. Walker would not take kindly to their mistreating the Indians."

"Yes," I said. "I can see that, once they concocted that story, they lacked the intelligence and grit to deny it."

"What we have to reckon is how to show that they lied."

He looked at me, but I had no ideas. I shook my head.

"I feel like Daniel being thrown into the lions' den for not praying to an earthly king," admitted Joshua. "At least he knew that God would send his angels to stop the lions' mouths. I wish I had that assurance."

I felt an idea stirring in my head, but I could not quite corral it.

Joshua said, "I wonder if Billy and Joseph will have any qualms about putting their hands on the Bible and bearing false witness?"

Daniel. False witness. Bible. It came back to me then.

"Is Father Stone still here?" I demanded.

"He was over by the grocery where they sell whiskey a moment ago," answered Joshua. "But I don't think he could get the trial stopped, if that's what you have in mind. He's too much of an Abolitionist for some men and not enough of one for others. Besides, he's a Catholic priest and some men will disregard him for that reason alone. He couldn't quiet the mob, try as he might."

"Stall for time till I find him and get what we need," I shouted over my shoulder as I struck out through the masses of people. I slipped and slithered my way until I spotted the priest. I practically knocked him down to get his attention.

"You have to help me prevent a terrible tragedy," I exclaimed. "I need to borrow a Roman Catholic Bible."

"Of course, but I don't know how it will help you. Catholic Bibles are like Protestant Bibles except they include what is called the Apocrypha. Those are books that were excluded from the Protestant canon...."

"Pardon me, Father, you can tell me all about it later," I said. "Right now I need to get ahold of one of those Bibles before this trial starts."

"I have one in my room in Mrs. Wilson's boardinghouse. I can get it for you, but it would not be proper for a young lady to come to my room without a chaperone..."

I grabbed his arm and pulled him through the crowd toward the boardinghouse. Once there, I rushed him up the steps and to his room.

"Where's one of those Bibles?" I asked. He pulled a thick book from a pile. I put it on the floor, dropped down on my hands and knees and flung the Bible open as quickly as reverence would allow. I found the story of Susanna and stuck a loose feather in the Bible to mark the place. The priest picked up another Bible. I grabbed his hand and hauled him back through the crowd.

As I pulled him through the assembled, Father Stone said, "That story is not in the Protestant Bible. I see why you need it, but how is it that a girl on the frontier knows about Biblical scholarship?"

"My father was a Congregational minister. My mother had us read and discuss the Apocrypha. She said we should know what other religions believe. She said we would benefit from the instruction. She didn't know how right she was."

We wove our way through the crowd back to the site of the trial.

While I was gone, men had erected a large wooden frame and stretched canvas over it for shade, making a kind of square tent with open sides. Wooden planks placed on two sawhorses on one side made a judge's bench. Next to the bench in the clear view of the jurors sat a plain wooden chair for witnesses. Chairs and benches sat on one side for the jurors. Across from them were chairs for Walker and his sons and for Joshua and me. Red Hawk and Buffalo Tracker sat on the ground near Joshua and me. Tom Evans sat behind them with a shotgun. Curious people huddled together outside in the sun all around the tent. Walker's horse and his sons' mustangs were tethered just outside the tent.

Mr. Carlson was looking at his pocket watch as we skidded to a stop.

"I found it," I said, holding up the Bible.

Carlson raised a carpenter's hammer and pounded on the makeshift bench. It made a loud hollow sound.

"T-t-time to start," said Carlson. "Mr. Walker, you go first."

Walker rose and addressed the jury.

"Gentlemen of the jury, I would first like to apologize and thank my young friend— friends who will defend the accused. I own that I was rash and impetuous when I, with others, attempted to hang the men accused without giving them a chance to defend themselves. I admit I have a terrible temper. I failed to keep it in check and I nearly did something I would have sorely regretted later on."

Walker paused for breath before continuing: "The enterprise we are now embarked upon is altogether different. I shall prove that the men in question did in fact commit a crime, the punishment for which is death. My worthy opponents shall attempt to defend them. It will be left to you gentlemen to determine their fate based upon what is demonstrated here. It is true that in the particular I am the aggrieved party. My horses were stolen. However, unlike the ill-conceived action rashly taken before, this trial is not an action taken in anger or for revenge. I represent the people of the territory. Any one of us might be robbed, and, as young Amy remarked, we all know that stealing a person's horse out here where there are hostile Indians, wild animals, prairie fires and dangerous weather may condemn that person to certain death. The penalty for stealing a horse is just and proportional to the seriousness of the crime."

The jurors nodded their heads, listening intently.

"I will today demonstrate beyond the reasonable doubt of any man that the Indians did attempt to steal horses and that by their actions they placed themselves in opposition to the laws of civilization and of the Kansas Territory. They have pulled down upon their own heads the weight of the law, and they will be punished, not in anger or revenge but in judicious response to the odious behavior that they chose to inflict upon the peace and welfare of the community."

Walker nodded to the jurors and sat down.

Joshua turned to me and said, "Go it, Amy."

I felt like someone had kicked me in the stomach. My jaw dropped and I stared at him. "You're the one who ponders in the family," I protested. "I'm the one who acts."

"You ran off with the priest and returned with books. You

have some idea of what to do. I do not. You have a good mind when you slow down enough to use it. Use it now, or Red Hawk and Buffalo Tracker will hang."

I closed my eyes. I said a short but fervent prayer. I called to mind the fine words I'd heard from Fourth of July speakers, the constitutional wrangles between free staters and slave staters and the speeches of lawyers on law days when we watched trials held in Manhattan. That served as high drama for us out here on the prairie. Then I stood up and commenced.

"Gentlemen of the jury," I choked out, "I must tell you that the responsibility of defending these men renders me nearly senseless." I took a breath. "I calm myself with the knowledge that you are responsible and sensible men who I can trust to attend to the evidence presented and make your decision upon that alone. Mr. Walker said he represents the people of the territory. He does, and so do I. He said any of you might be robbed. I say any of you might be accused of robbery and find yourself in a situation where you need to rely on the wisdom of your fellow citizens. You could also rely on one thing more. As we have all heard lawyers say during trials, the accused does not have to prove that he is innocent. The accusers have to prove he is guilty. If the proof offered is not wholly convincing, if a reasonable man might doubt any single part of the case against the accused, then you must give a verdict of not guilty. Please bear in mind that you need not say a man is innocent. You can say that his guilt is not proven. It is that and your wisdom that I rely upon."

Sweating and trembling, I collapsed into my chair

Joshua patted me on my sweaty shoulder and said, "Very well done."

"Well done? I've barely started. We have to talk to the judge before the testimony starts."

I picked up the Bible and cantered over to the bench. I waved for Father Stone to join us. Joshua followed, looking at me with obvious curiosity. Walker came over, frowning.

"Billy and Joseph are the only witnesses, aren't they, Mr. Walker?" I asked.

Walker nodded.

"Your honor, I have a request that I believe will help the jurors come to a fair and valid verdict. It will pose no hardship on Mr. Walker but will establish the credibility of the witnesses beyond question."

"What do you propose and why?" asked Walker.

"I propose that each of your witnesses should be removed from the area while the other witness is testifying. I suggest that each witness should give his account without knowing what the other witness said. If each witness recounts the same testimony without knowing what the other said, it is a strong argument that they are telling the truth. That could be detrimental to my clients, but we are interested in the truth. If, on the other hand, they give different accounts of the events, it will be strong evidence that they are lying. I am willing to risk it, Mr. Walker. What about you?"

"I've never heard of such a thing," said Walker. "What is your authority for making for such a strange request?"

"Holy Scripture," answered Father Stone, perhaps seeing the chance to stop the shedding of innocent blood. "Miss Gregson recalled the story of Susanna, another virtuous young woman somewhat older than herself. Two elders demanded that she lie with them or they would accuse her of being with a young man under a tree in her garden. Trusting in God, she refused and was tried for adultery. Daniel, the stalwart of the Lord, defended her. He separated the false accusers and asked each one what kind of tree the couple had been under. Each accuser gave a different answer, and thus they proved themselves to be liars. You may remember Daniel. It was he who was later cast into the lions' den. Protected by angels, he emerged unscathed. When his accusers were thrown to the lions, they were savaged and eaten. Here are the appropriate passages."

Walker read the passages quickly. Then he read them again slowly twice while Carlson plodded through the words. Carlson closed the Bible and sat quietly for a moment.

"I thought I knew most Bible stories, but I don't recall this one," said Walker. "What book of the Bible is it in?"

"It's in the Apocrypha," answered the priest.

"Bailiff," called Carlson, "separate the witnesses and keep them far enough away that they cannot hear what is being said in court until I send for them. Mr. Walker, are you ready to begin?"

Walker looked as though he might protest, but he knew he could not oppose Scripture.

"Yes, your honor," said Walker. "I call Billy Walker to the stand."

I noted that when Billy was called upon to put his hand upon a Bible and swear that he would tell the truth, he barely touched the Bible with his fingertips. He looked from side to side as if seeking guidance. I suspicioned that Joseph, the younger brother, was the leader of the two. I tucked away that information for future use.

Asked to swear, Billy mumbled something inaudible.

"W-What was that?" asked Carlson. "I could not hear you."

"I do," said Billy.

Walker conducted a very short examination. Billy said he

and his brother caught the Indians trying to steal horses. He said he and Joseph returned the horses to the barn and locked it tight before heading toward Manhattan with the would-be thieves. He said they rode their mustangs and made the Indians walk so they could not get away. They met their father on the trail. Walker concluded, "I have no more questions." He sat down.

I was surprised to find myself feeling sorry for Billy. Joshua nudged me. "You've done well so far. If I start now, it will just confuse the jury."

I felt fear creeping in again, but I had to admit that Joshua was right. I stood up and strode toward the witness.

Billy blinked rapidly as I approached him. "Did you concoct the fairy tale about the Indians, or was that Joseph?"

"What do you mean?" he asked.

"When you and Joseph saw your pa coming along to where you'd been tormenting the Indians, was it you or Joseph who thought you'd avoid a whipping if you claimed they'd been trying to steal horses?"

"How did you know that?" asked Billy. "I mean, they were trying to steal the horses."

"When you two lied about them, did you even think that they might get hanged?"

"No! I mean we didn't lie about them." Sweat rolled down Billy's face.

"Let's continue this tall tale if we must," I said. "When did you and your brother first see the Indians?"

"When?"

"Yes, when?"

"Today."

People in the audience laughed.

"When today?"

"Um, early in the morning," said Billy.

"Where did you two see them?"

Billy hesitated. "They were sneaking around outside our horse barn."

"You were able to see them even though they were sneaking? Well done. It's hard to find Indians when they don't want to be seen."

Billy looked down. I continued. "Where were your horses?"

"They were inside the barn."

"If the Indians were outside the barn and the horses were inside, how do you know the Indians were trying to steal the horses?"

Billy was silent for some time. He looked at the people around him. Finally he said, "Later on, nigh to noon, we saw them lead two horses out of the barn."

"Which two horses?"

Billy squirmed. He squinted and wrinkled his brow. Once again he looked at the people around him before answering in a rush, "General Washington and General Lafayette."

"Is there some reason, Billy, why you take so long to answer simple questions like when and where you saw the Indians and what horses they took? Are you making up the answers after I ask the questions?"

Billy hung his head.

"Never mind," I said. "You don't need to answer that. I don't want you to lie any more than you have to."

Again the audience laughed.

"The Generals are a team, aren't they, Billy?"

"The best horse team in the territory at breaking the prairie or hauling a heavy load," he said.

"Yes," I agreed. "They are the biggest, strongest horses I've ever seen. They work steadily until the job gets done. Of course, I've never known Indians to plow land or freight heavy loads in wagons. Have you?"

"No."

"Then, with all the horses to choose from, Billy, why do you suppose the Indians chose two that do things of no value to them?"

Billy did not answer.

"Unless, of course the Indians did not take any horses at all. Were the Generals the first horses you happened to think of after I asked my question? Is that it?"

"No."

"When your father saw you two boys on the trail, where were you taking the Indians?"

"To Manhattan."

"I have no further questions."

Walker declined to ask Billy anything else. Len Haskin took Billy out of earshot. Zachary Bailey brought in Joseph. Joseph walked in with his head erect, sat down in the chair, placed his hand firmly on the Bible and in a loud clear voice promised to tell the truth.

When Walker rose to question his son, I saw anger in his eyes. He asked why Joseph and Billy had been with the Indians.

"They were trying to steal our horses."

Then Walker said, "I have no more questions."

When I approached Joseph, he settled back in the chair in a relaxed posture, putting his hands together behind his head. I paused to look at him. There was a mocking expression on his handsome face. I noted that his hair was neatly trimmed, and, unusual for the territory, his clothing was store-bought and altered so it fit him well.

"Joseph," I asked, "it was you that came up with this elaborate fib, wasn't it?"

"Whatever do you mean?" asked Joseph, grinning at me.

"When you saw your father approaching, you knew he'd whip the tar out of you for bedeviling the Indians, right? Wasn't it you who thought that if you boys accused the Indians of stealing horses, he'd get so upset at them that he wouldn't beat you? Billy couldn't think of something like that, could he?"

"No, he couldn't," said Joseph. "I mean, no, we weren't fibbing."

"When did you boys first see the Indians?"

Joseph answered immediately, "'Bout one o'clock or one thirty in the afternoon."

"You're certain of the time?"

"Absolutely."

"Where were the Indians when the two of you first saw them?"

"They were on the trail maybe a sixteenth of a mile or so from our farm."

"You're certain of the place?"

"I am."

"What were they doing?"

"They were leading two of our horses, trying to make off with them. I reckon they were walking the horses to keep them quiet until they got far enough away from our place that they could ride 'em. That's how come me and Billy could catch them on our horses." Joseph puffed out his chest. "Even though they were full-grown men, Billy and me forced them to take the horses back to our barn. We locked the barn so no other horses could get out and then we set out to bring the Indians in. We rode our mustangs and made the Indians walk so they could not get away."

"Which two horses did the Indians take?"

"They took Twister and Prairie Fire, the fastest horses between here and the Rocky Mountains."

"You're certain about the horses?"

"I know our horses."

"And where were you taking the Indians when you met your father?"

"We were headed to Fort Riley to turn the Indians in when my pa found us."

"You're certain about your destination?"

"I am."

I paused, wondering if the jury had noted the differences between the accounts given by Billy and Joseph. I looked over at Joshua, who winked at me.

Walker fidgeted in his chair. He made as if to rise twice before he stood up. His face was pale and his voice was shaky when he spoke, "I ask the court to direct the jury to return a verdict of not guilty. It is clear that my sons are lying. I apologize to the court, to the people of Manhattan and to the two Indians in particular. I apologize for my rash actions and temper. I apologize for my sons in whom I am deeply and profoundly disappointed."

For the first time, Joseph looked frightened. He jumped off the chair and ran into the crowd, dodging spectators as he sped away.

Carlson pounded his hammer on the bench. "Case dismissed. The accused are free to go."

The jurors looked at each other in surprise. Some men stomped off in search of a drink. One man appealed to his neighbors that Billy and Joseph should be tried and then hanged. Joshua signed to Red Hawk and Buffalo Tracker that they would not hang. They nodded and seemed content to stay seated where they were. Tom Evans, standing behind them, announced, "I always knew they were innocent."

Under the canvas, people from the audience surged, talking and gesturing to each other. Walker stared ahead, looking at nothing. People moved around him, leaving him alone in an open space. Joshua and I pulled away from people congratulating us and approached him.

"Mr. Walker," said Joshua, "asking for a verdict of not guilty was a courageous and honest thing."

Walker blinked and looked down at us. Anger, embarrassment and sadness washed over his features in quick succession. He took a deep breath before speaking.

"Thank you, Joshua. It needed to be done." He looked at me. "Congratulations, young lady. Thank you both for saving me from doing a terrible wrong. I need to talk with the Indians."

We walked over to Red Hawk and Buffalo Tracker and sat down to talk with them. Walker signed an apology and offered to replace anything they had lost. They dickered for a while until both sides agreed. Walker handed over two silver dollars. As we stood up to leave, an idea occurred to me. I signed to the Indians to wait.

"Mr. Walker, sir," I said, "if I may ask, how do you intend to punish your sons?"

"I don't know. I've nearly worn out a leather strap on them, but it doesn't seem to help. I suppose I could get a new strap."

"Meaning no criticism, sir," said Joshua, "I'm not certain that doing more of what didn't work before is likely to help now.

Kansas Justice

Perhaps if they had been less fearful, they might have been more honest. It seems to me that they constructed a lie full of quicksand and then could not get unstuck from it."

"There might be a way to get their attention and to make recompense to Red Hawk and Buffalo Tracker for their suffering," I said.

"I need to do that," said Walker.

"Joseph and Billy talked about the Indians stealing horses, sir," I said. "Billy said they took a team, but they have no need for horses to plow a field or haul freight. Joseph said they took racers. I'm sure the Indians would like fast horses, but your racers need to be fed grain from time to time, which would be hard to come by where the Indians are headed."

Joshua caught on immediately. "Of course, sir, there are horses that can survive on what they forage for themselves. They aren't the fastest horses or the strongest but they're tough and they have great endurance."

"Mustangs," said Walker. "Born and bred in the wild, they would be best for the Indians. You know, come to think of it, I believe my boys would see the world differently on foot than they did from the backs of those horses."

When we left Manhattan to head home, Billy and Joseph had not been found but Walker assured us he was not worried about them.

"They're hiding out and punishing themselves in their imaginations worse than anything I could ever do to them. They'll come home when they get hungry enough. They'll think about what they did all the way home. And they'll be walking."

Joshua and I headed home. I thought about all that had happened. When my ma first got together with Joshua's pa, I wasn't excited about having him as a stepbrother. I could fight

35

harder, run faster and shoot straighter than he could, even though he was a year older than me. He took after his father in that he didn't look like much, but nobody ever said he wasn't smart. Put him to a task and he would labor until the task was completed. Seeing Joshua stand alone against the mob made me feel proud to be his sister.

"How did you feel when you stood up against the mob?" I asked him.

"I was so scared I thought I'd pee in my breeches," he said.

"I was so scared that I froze up. I couldn't think of anything to do."

"How did you feel when you stood up in court to defend Red Hawk and Buffalo Tracker?" asked Joshua.

"I thought my knees would buckle and I would fall down."

"You thought of a defense. I was completely out of powder and shot," said Joshua.

"You know, for a brother, you're not half bad."

"Thank you. For a sister, you're nearly tolerable," said Joshua.

Author's note: This story was accepted for an anthology, but the entire anthology was scrapped due to finances so this is the story's first time in print.

Butterfly Milkweed

Kansas Territory near the Taylor Farm, May 11, 1856

Time slows and then stops. Worry, doubt, hope and fear all fall away from my mind, leaving me with one terrible, clear certainty: In this place, at this time, I will die. Here on the hilltop, alone, surrounded by enemies, I will die. My heartbeat roars in my ears. I grip the sharp edges of the flint spearhead hidden in my hand, coiling myself to explode from my kneeling position. In a second, Dakota will drop his hand toward his gun. I will strike upward, howling, and rip his throat open. His hot blood will spurt out. Maybe I will be able to seize his gun in the seconds before the others react. Maybe not. Either way, the others will blast away at me until my body is shot to pieces. I will die today, but I will not die alone.

The sky is bright with a few wispy clouds. From the hilltop I can see rolling green hills and a clear unlimited horizon. The prairie flowers have erupted into crimson, yellow, orange and blue. They sweeten the air. I smell smoke from the fire and the sweat of horses. I can hear a stream tumbling down the hillside. It is this image etched into my brain that I will carry into eternity.

Someone lands on my back, followed quickly by another. The laughter of children dissolves the memory and brings me back to the present. I struggle back into being civilized like a man forcing himself into a nightshirt too small for him.

"Got you!" shouted Joshua. "Admit it. You didn't hear us sneaking up on you until we pounced."

"If we were Indians, we would have captured you," said Amy.

I stood up with the laughing children hanging on me. Joshua was my son. I had a private dream that Amy would be my daughter, if I ever got up the courage to ask her mother to marry me, and if her mother was foolish enough to accept. I bent down again and they slid off.

"That was very good," I said. "I didn't hear a thing. You kept out of my line of sight and approached downwind so I couldn't hear or smell you. I got caught up in a memory of what happened here several years ago. I wasn't paying attention."

"What did happen here, Pa?" asked Joshua. "You were a hundred miles away in your thoughts."

"Wait!" commanded Amy. "Mr. Miller, Joshua says knowing about flowers could save my life someday. That can't be true, can it?"

I answered, "When Joshua tells you something that you don't know, he rubs it in. It's not fair. He's lived here most of his life, and you just arrived. If we were back in Boston, you would be the teacher and he would be the student. On the other hand, I've not heard him lie to you about anything and he's gentler about it than most would be."

Amy said, "When I first got here, he let me lead him into the prairie and then he asked me to show the way back. He let me walk in circles for a long time. Home was just over the hill."

"You know the Walker boys would have led you into the prairie and run off, leaving you alone, lost and crying. Joshua wanted to show you that you have to pay close attention to the lay of the land to keep from getting lost. There are no roads on the prairie. If you find a trail, you don't know if it will lead to the next farm or if it will fade away in the middle of nowhere. So many places hereabouts look alike that even people who have lived here for a long time can easily get lost. Joshua stayed with you and you learned a survival lesson. You're getting to be as fast as he is and nearly as strong. I have the feeling that pretty soon you will be better than he is at a lot of things. We'll see how you act when the shoe is on the other foot."

Amy stuck her tongue out at Joshua. One of the things I liked about her was that she would not be buffaloed.

"Knowing about flowers can save your life. It certainly saved mine. Let me tell you about what happened here." I swallowed and continued: "I've been meaning to tell you for some time."

I was out gathering herbs for medicine on a day like this one but later in the summer when the men came upon me at this very spot. They emerged from the trees as silently as deer. I knew I was in trouble. There were eight of them riding tired but well-muscled horses. The men were well armed, unshaven and caked with dirt from unceasing travel. Several had bloodied swathes of cloth wrapped around wounds. Riding far off the trails, they did not expect to meet anyone. They stared at me grimly, clearly not pleased to see me. My rifle was slung over my back by a strap. I had a small knife in my hand that I used to dig up roots and harvest plants.

Most of the men were young. Marauders usually don't live long. One man, older than the rest and with gray in his hair, asked, "What are you doing here?"

"Gathering herbs for medicine." I held up the root I had

been cleaning.

He pointed to my horse hitched to a tree. "Is that swayback yours?"

"He is. He gets me where I want to go— eventually."

The other men laughed. All but one, that is. A dark-skinned, blue-eyed handsome young man, not much older than Joshua is now, urged his horse forward and drew a pistol.

"Hold off, Dakota," said the older man.

"He's seen us, Lee," said Dakota. "I don't like witnesses."

Lee said, "I don't like shooting when we don't know who's around to hear it. Anybody who comes to see why shots were fired is going to find our trail. We've worked too hard to cover our tracks to throw that away by foolishness."

Dakota turned to face Lee. "Who are you calling a fool?" he asked, staring at Lee as unblinking as a snake. Lee looked back without showing concern, but I sensed he was uneasy. At a guess, I would have said that the tension between them had been building for some time.

A bearded man dressed in rags said, "Dakota, you've been bragging about your knife fighting. Why don't you shuck them pistols and go after him afoot? We ain't had no entertainment for weeks." Several men voiced their approval and spurred their horses forward into a semicircle. They joked and smiled. Some-one called out a bet on Dakota. Another man bet on me. Some men encouraged Dakota, while others taunted him. I leaned my rifle against a tree. Lee said nothing. I wondered if he wanted me to kill Dakota or if he wanted Dakota to kill me. Then the biggest man I ever saw came riding up, leading what I took at first glance for a packhorse. He had black hair and eyes, a flat-tened nose and a half-grown-out beard.

"What's goin' on here?" the big man asked.

The bearded man chuckled. "We're about to see if Dakota can skin him an herbalist or if he's gonna get himself skinned."

"An herbalist?" the big man asked. He looked at me. "Are you a doctor?"

"No, I'm a farmer, but I've done my share of doctoring."

"My name is David. I'd like you to take a look at my brother, Jonathon. He's in a bad way." David looked at Dakota. "You can fight him after you come through me."

Dakota spat and turned away. The other men drifted off.

What I had initially taken for a packhorse load turned out to be a slender, young blond man slumped over and tied to his saddle. David untied him and lifted him tenderly to the ground.

Jonathon was in bad shape. He looked way too young to be with this wolf pack, his face not showing even a hint of whiskers. His skin was pale and slick with sweat. His breathing was shallow. He was barely conscious. When I peeled away his shirt, I found that a bandage wrapped around his upper arm was soaked with blood. There was a bullet crease along the side of his abdomen, but that was scabbed over nicely. Removing his breeches, I found that his left thigh had been shot through. The bandage there was also soaked with blood.

"How is he?" asked David.

"Not good." I trickled some water from my canteen into Jonathan's mouth and he swallowed it.

"Will he die?"

"I don't know. I've seen men hurt worse who survived and men not hurt as badly who died. The bullets that went through him didn't hit any arteries or shatter any bones. Otherwise he'd be dead already. But bouncing on the horse has kept the wounds open. He could bleed out like a butchered hog. I know he's tough because he's still alive. If you keep him still, he has a chance to live. If you keep him moving, he will die."

David said, "Lee won't split money from the job until we get to where we're going."

I said, "You can ride on with the rest and I'll take care of your brother."

Lee spoke from behind us. Obviously he'd been listening the whole time. "Sorry, David, I can't allow that. The local sheriff would hear about a man shot up like Jonathon is. The law would be on our trail again. We've had fresh horses three times now, so if the posse is still looking for us they're at least five or six days behind us. Nobody hereabouts is looking for us. I won't give up that advantage." He paused. "Tell you what I'll do, though. The men and animals need a rest. We can stop for a day or so, have the farmer tend our wounds, and scout out fresh mounts. We'll see how your brother does with some rest and doctoring."

Lee looked at me. "I don't suppose you'd tell us where we could find good horses around here."

I said nothing.

Lee said, "I didn't think so."

Lee organized camp, picking out places where a man could see all approaches and setting a schedule for guard duty. He set some men to dig a latrine and others to clear away brush from under a tall tree. Smoke from a fire lit there would disperse through the branches. Dakota did not object when Lee assigned him to picket the horses. I waited until Lee had everyone working before approaching him.

"I'm going to need to gather more herbs to tend to your wounded. If someone could start heating water in a couple of pots while I'm gone, that would help."

Lee asked, "What else do you need?"

"Rolls of cloth. Pots and pans. Empty bottles if you've got them and whatever medicine your men carry." I thought for a moment. "Some whiskey if you've got any."

Lee raised his eyebrows.

"Not for me to drink. It can cut the bitter taste of herbs. Men who won't swallow medicine by itself will drink it in whiskey."

Lee searched me for weapons. He allowed me my knife. He assigned David to watch me and carry for me, knowing he would not let me out of his sight. Most of what I needed grew by stream banks. Other plants I collected needed open space to thrive.

"How do you know about plants?" David asked.

"I'm a farmer. I've learned to tell whether shoots coming up are weeds or crops. My friend, Spotted Calf, showed me the plants his tribe uses. Indians have been on this land for a long time. They know a lot that we don't. Consider this plant with a long stem and a single flower. It grows in dry sunny spots. The flower has an orange ball, and purple petals grow down from the ball like a lady's parasol. It's called a coneflower. Indians use it to treat hard-to-heal wounds and breathing problems. Most White folks think it's just a weed."

I harvested the flower.

"I also helped Doc Bradley during the fever outbreak. He uses plants as well as medicine from back east. He insists that keeping wounds clean and boiling bandages before using them saves lives. I've heard other doctors call him a fool, but when their wives and children get sick, they send for him."

"My brother made friends with the Indians back home," said David. "He was always off hunting with them or doing some fool thing."

43

Murder Manhattan Style

"He might be interested in this," I said, pointing. I gingerly dug a piece of flint out of the mud. "See, it's been shaped around the sides and the point. Indians have been coming here for hundreds of years to make arrowheads and spearheads. I don't know when this was started but it's sharp enough to pierce a buffalo hide. It's too big to be an arrowhead, it must have been intended for a spear."

David said, "Can we take it back to show him?"

"Sure thing." Taking care not to cut myself, I cleaned the mud from the spearhead in the stream and slipped it into one of the sacks.

Back in camp, we found that a low fire of dried wood was burning. I noted with approval that two coffee pots half full of water sat on the embers. Other pots and pans were close at hand. I lined up about half a dozen sacks of various sizes full of herbs, checking the contents of each one. Dakota stood close by, sneering at me. I retrieved the flint spearhead unobtrusively just before he came over.

"What do you have in the sacks?" he demanded.

"Herbs. The short plant with four angled leaves is called heal-all for its medicinal properties. Others are named for their shape. There's thorn apple, lion's tooth and coneflowers. The one with hooded blue flowers is called skullcap. And there are other herbs."

He noticed that I had skipped a sack.

"What's in that one?" he said, pointing to the sack I'd skipped. He grabbed the bag. "Are you hiding something in here?"

"I wouldn't do that," I warned.

That was all the reason Dakota needed to plunge his hand deeply into the sack. He howled like a wild animal and dropped

44

it. The sack of stinging nettles fell to the ground. Dakota danced and waved his hand through the air, trying to dislodge the nettles that had fastened to his hand and wrist. When the last nettle fell off, he held his hand in front of his face and watched it swell and redden. I crouched on the ground, the spearhead hidden in my hand. I felt layers of civilization peel away from me. In a moment, my enemy would drop his hand toward his gun. I would strike, tearing open his throat as I sang my death song. I never felt more alive than on this beautiful day. I would die today but I would not die alone.

I locked eyes with Dakota.

He said, "I'm going to kill you."

I launched myself at him as he dropped his hand.

Something heavy blasted me below my ribs. It knocked me sideways as the spearhead went spinning away. I landed on my face and tasted blood. A heavy weight pinned me down despite the rage that coursed through my blood. I struggled but I could not escape.

Dakota shouted, "Move or I'll shoot through you!"

I heard a chopping sound. Dakota collapsed in a heap.

I was confused and annoyed to find myself alive, panting and sweating under a heavy burden that I could not shift.

"Take it easy," whispered David in my ear. "It's all over. Lee clipped Dakota with his gun barrel. He's out cold."

I was pinned underneath David. I said, "You can get off me now." David rolled off. I stayed on the ground for a moment, gathering myself. When I stood, wincing in pain, I noticed two men dragging Dakota away.

"Did you kill him?" I asked Lee.

"I thought about it, but I didn't."

"You should have."

I cleaned Jonathon's wounds and applied a poultice of heal-all. I wrapped him with clean bandages and noted a slight improvement in his color. I put a few stinging nettle leaves in a shallow pan and poured boiling water over them. Then I carefully peeled away the outside layer. I put the inner material in a pot. I left the spikes and exterior skin in the pan. I soaked the inner material in cold water and examined it closely to be certain it was clear of stickers.

I explained to David. "As hard as it is to get to, the inside of the nettle, properly cleaned, is an excellent food for sick or injured people. You can chop it up into tiny pieces and feed Jonathon a little at a time in a broth. Keep giving him a trickle of cold water frequently, too. He needs to replace the blood he's lost."

When I finished with Jonathon, I started to look at other men who had been wounded. Fortunately, none of their wounds had begun to putrefy. For the rest of the day and all the day that followed, I cleaned wounds, wrapped them in fresh bandages and told the men to keep the wounds clean. I made several trips for fresh herbs. After a little while, I was allowed to come and go on my own. A few of the men had coughs so I made a tea for them to drink from cone flowers, bee balm and a sprinkle of pulverized thorn apple seeds. I set a couple of pots simmering with other herbal teas. I made a poultice from evening primrose roots and coneflowers for the men's sores.

I told David to add some chopped up lion's tooth root (some call it dandelion) to the stinging nettle broth he fed to his brother.

David said, "Jonathon woke up for a minute today for the first time in a week or more. I've been keeping him clean, and he's looking better. He was as weak as a newborn kitten, but the bleeding has stopped. I reckon you saved his life."

I looked over at Jonathon. He was sleeping.

"He looks better," I agreed. "In another week or so, he should be able to straddle a horse and ride slowly without endangering his life."

David went from happy to glum. "I don't know how much longer we'll stay here. The horses have nearly recovered and the men are getting restless. Lee had them digging rifle pits around the perimeter. Between you and me, I suspect that's mostly to keep them busy. Everybody pulls sentry duty. He's got scouts out on patrol day and night with orders to watch but not to shoot. So far all they've seen are a few Indians. Our horses are better than what we've seen around here."

"I hadn't thought on it, but I imagine he doesn't want this bunch to have idle time on their hands. They'd probably turn on each other out of boredom. I wonder if he used to be an army officer."

Lee's voice came from behind us. "Hell, no. I've always worked for a living. I admit that I was a sergeant once before the lure of whiskey and easy money ended my career."

"Is that when you learned to be where nobody expects you?"

Lee said, "Yep, it keeps the men on their toes thinking that I might be out there watching them at any time. Dakota's hand is just now getting back to normal size. I thought I'd warn you."

David said, "You should have killed him. He's working up steam to come after you."

"Maybe so," said Lee. "But the farmer here is first on his list. Dakota is hell on wheels once the shooting starts. He's probably too stupid to realize that he can get killed. Once I saw him ride right over a woman carrying a crying baby because she

47

didn't get out of his way quick enough. You can't be too choosy when you put together a gang to rob banks. Some of the men think he'd be a better leader than I am. Never you mind that he couldn't plan for a robbery of a one-room schoolhouse or figure his way out of a gunny sack."

David told Lee, "Jonathon's better, but he can't travel. I'd like to leave him here with the herbalist."

I said, "It will be about a week before he can travel safely on horseback. I'll stay with him. Your men and animals are in shape to travel again. You'd be long gone before I had a chance to go to the sheriff. Leave me afoot without a weapon if you like."

Lee tilted his head to one side as he considered the proposal. "Dakota would circle back to kill you if I did that. If you hid, he'd torture Jonathon to bring you out of hiding."

David said, "Let me take care of Dakota."

Lee shook his head. "Likely you and Dakota would both die, and I can't afford that. I need at least one of you to keep the others in line. Can you handle Dakota, Farmer?"

"Not with guns," I admitted. "But there is a way. Do you want to throw a going-away jubilee?"

I explained my plan to Lee. Ex-military man that he was, he made several tactical changes. I knew that old Ben Schuler kept a still not far from here. He usually had a couple jugs of whiskey there. Lee and David came with me to see that I did not tamper with the whiskey beforehand. They watched while I poured a cup of strong tea into one half-filled jug. I shook it to mix the tea with the whiskey. Lee made me take a swallow to prove that it would not kill me. In a few minutes I felt feverish and the light hurt my eyes.

"I'll survive. It is bitter. Will that bother Dakota?"

"As long as it's whiskey, he won't mind," said Lee.

"If he drinks the whole jug, it will knock him out. You'll have to tie him to a horse to get him away from here. You can keep him tied up until he's far away. "

They found four other jugs. Lee reckoned that his men could drink half a jug each and barely feel a thing. When we got back to camp, he showed the men the jugs. He promised that once the rifle pits were filled in and the horses and equipment passed inspection, the men could finish off the whiskey before they rode out.

Dakota was the first one to present himself for inspection. Lee looked over his horse and weapons, pronounced them ready and gave him the jug I had doctored. Dakota wrapped his arms around it and snarled at anyone who dared to come close to him. Knowing his moods, the other men left him alone. Dakota fixed me with a hard stare between greedy swallows. Once, when he thought Lee was not looking, he drew his finger across his throat in a slashing motion. He drained the jug, clutched his throat and staggered off in the direction of the latrine. The other men were too busy drinking to notice.

When the first man sitting on the grass fell backward to the ground there was some consternation, but when he started to snore loudly, the rest of the men laughed and finished off the jugs. One by one the men fell asleep. Lee did not start drinking until every man passed inspection. He tried to hold himself erect by sheer will. He was the last one to topple.

I checked Dakota first. He was stretched out on the ground, dead. I tried to dredge up a feeling of remorse for killing him but I could not. I was sorry about his wasted life, but sorrier about the pain he had caused others. I asked God for forgiveness for not feeling guilty and then went to check on the others.

Everyone else was sleeping. One by one I removed their weapons, rolled them on their backs and trussed their wrists together. I removed their boots and hobbled them at the ankles and knees. They looked like calves ready to be branded. I worked slowly enough to be certain with every knot.

"What did you put in the whiskey?" asked a familiar voice. I looked up to see an old friend.

"Hello, Spotted Calf. Somebody mentioned seeing Indians. I wondered if you were around. I made strong skullcap tea. Every time it was ready I put some in a small bottle, snuck over to old Ben's still and poured it into one of the jugs. The men were used to seeing pots of tea simmering. Luckily nobody poured himself a cup while I was gone."

"Good choice," he said. "That could put the whole U.S. cavalry to sleep. How'd you kill the madman?"

"I made a special tea from thorn apple seeds and poured it into the jug for him. The outlaw leader made me take a swig. I didn't swallow much, but it still got me feverish."

"Jimsonweed seeds are especially poisonous," said Spotted Calf. "Strong medicine for a strong evil spirit—jimsonweed, thorn apple; I've heard it called devil's trumpet, too. It called him to hell. Too bad he died so quickly."

"Would you mind going to tell the sheriff where I am?"

"He's on his way already," he answered. "He should be here soon. I'll be gone by then. The sheriff and I are not friends. He's from back east. He doesn't understand our ways. The bad men rode good horses. Do you think anybody would notice if a few went missing?"

"Leave the tack behind. They robbed a bank so there should be money in some of the saddlebags. Nobody's going to care about horses, but I'd hate to have a posse chasing you."

Butterfly Milkweed

"Ha! You'd hate to be in the posse that chases me. I'll leave everything but the horses." Spotted Calf left as quietly as he had come.

Sheriff Seth Child arrived shortly thereafter.

"Lizzie sent me to find you," he said. "She probably got tired of doing your share of the chores."

"Most likely."

Child noticed the men tied up on the ground and snoring.

"What have we here, Benjamin?" he asked.

"Bank robbers from somewhere back to the east," I answered. "If you get a wagon, we could toss 'em in the back and carry them to Fort Riley."

He looked around with a frown on his face.

"Why are they all asleep?"

"Because I didn't want to kill more of them than I had to."

Child looked at me. I stared back at him. Spotted Calf was right. Sometimes people from Massachusetts think every problem can be solved by words. Westerners know better.

I challenged him. "I did kill one of them. Do you want to arrest me?"

A wind rippled through the prairie grasses while the sheriff looked at me silently.

"You against a gang of bank robbers. How many were there?"

"Ten."

"Ten against one. No, I don't see any reason to arrest you. Where's the money?"

"Damned if I know. I was busy just staying alive."

"Point taken," said Child. "Why don't we toss 'em over their horses and tie them down? We could lead the horses back into town."

51

"We could if there are enough horses left."

"Was that damned Spotted Calf here? I thought I saw him in the shadows. He thinks it's funny to steal horses from me."

I smiled for the first time in what felt like a century. Child managed to take four men and all the loose tack on the five horses that Spotted Calf left us. He didn't find much money and he gave me a measuring look. I didn't care. He returned shortly with two more men and a wagon. Lee, David and the rest of the men came awake as we loaded them, still hogtied, into the wagon. We moved Jonathon carefully. The men fell silent when we tossed Dakota's body in with them.

The sheriff asked me, "Why did you kill him?"

Lee answered for me. "Dakota would have come back here sooner or later. The farmer humiliated him; worse than that, he wasn't fearful of him. Dakota wouldn't let that ride. He wouldn't have hesitated to burn down the farmer's house with his family inside or to sneak in and poison his well to get back at him. I should have remembered what a man with a family will do to protect them. I've been an outlaw too long. I should have killed Dakota myself and left Jonathon with the farmer."

I gathered up my herbs, my old horse and my rifle and headed back to Joshua and his mother, Lizzie. I had the taste of ashes in my mouth. I left home on a fool's errand. Nothing Spotted Calf, Doc Bradley or I could do would cure Lizzie's cough. No herb or medicine could add even a day to the little time she had left this world. Nothing could replace the days I lost by being away from her.

I looked at Joshua and Amy.

"Sheriff Child came by days later to tell me that most of the money from the bank robbery was recovered from the bodies of four outlaws cut down trying to get out of the town they robbed. The robbery left two townsmen dead and four wounded in the streets. The sheriff said an outlaw's horse knocked down a woman and her baby, but they were only bruised. The outlaws made off with about two hundred dollars."

"So that was why there wasn't much money in the saddle-bags," said Amy.

"And why Lee didn't want to divvy up the money before he had to," added Joshua.

"Yes, he was having trouble controlling the men already. If they found out how little money there was, they might have come after him."

"Did Jonathon recover?" asked Amy.

"He did. He was identified as one of the men who stayed outside the bank to control the horses. He was shot while holding a horse for his brother. He was sentenced to prison but only for four years. At trial some of the men claimed they were trying to get money for the pro-slavery cause. I think the jury knew that was just a poor excuse."

I paused. "I told you the story, Amy, so you could tell your ma the kind of man I really am. I still don't feel guilty for killing Dakota. I left my wife during her last days on a fool's errand. When I was down on the ground, ready to kill Dakota, I became just as much an animal as he was. I've never felt entirely civilized since then."

Joshua said, "You're the kind of man who came back to us even though the devil himself tried to stop you. I know as long as you have breath in your body, you always will."

Amy said, "You're the kind of man who saved Jonathon when it would have been easier to let him die. You could have poisoned all the robbers, but you didn't. You weren't tempted by money from the robbery and at the end of the day you didn't ride into town to brag on how clever you'd been. You just went home."

I shook my head. They didn't understand. They thought I was almost some kind of hero. I knew I was not. Amy's mother would see me for the fool I am.

Amy asked, "What kind of plant is that pretty one?"

"That's called a butterfly milkweed. Most of the year, it doesn't look like anything special. You hardly notice it until it flowers. Then it is pretty. Flowers can be any shade from yellow to deep orange. It attracts every kind of bee and butterfly that wants nectar. The Indians use it for throat and lung problems, fevers, cuts and sores. It's a good neighbor to other plants and doesn't spread to where it's not wanted. I'm told it grows all across the continent."

Amy said, "I'll tell Ma the story. She can draw her own conclusions."

The Great Manhattan
Mystery Conclave III

In 2006 the Great Manhattan Mystery Conclave honored Manhattan, Kansas-born Damon Runyon, whose short stories inspired the Broadway musical "Guys and Dolls." Just for fun I put up the following notice on my website:

The Great Manhattan Mystery Conclave III
I am sitting in Mindy's Restaurant at about one in the morning, shaking my head as I read yesterday's racing form. I wonder how any publication can possibly stay in business when it is so full of lies and false information dangerous to the financial health of gentlemen of the horse racing persuasion. Of course, I am reading yesterday's racing form because it is too early in the morning to pop for today's edition.

Sammy the Swami comes in and lays his latest prediction on the crowd. For once, I have to agree with him that it is a sure thing.

He says there is a shindig called "The Great Manhattan Mystery Conclave" taking place November 3-5, 2006, at the Ramada Plaza Hotel in Manhattan (Kansas, of course. Don't get confused. Find more information at *http://www.manhattanmysteries.com/*). It starts at nine in the morning on Friday, so you can just stay up from the night before and take a gander at the Book Babes – **Susan McBride** (the Debutant Dropout series), **Laura Durham** (the Wedding Planner series), and **Harley Jane Kozak** (*Dating Dead Men*), who are three of the best-looking gals who ever wore shoe leather. They'll tell you everything you wanted to know about publishing but were afraid to ask. Then **J.A. Konrath** (the Jacqueline "Jack" Daniel series) and **Rob Walker** (author of 41 books to date), two guys so tough that they wear out their clothes from the inside, will tell you about suspense and writing thrillers. I hear they're making a list of people who don't show. I wouldn't want to be on that list.

Saturday starts with **Nancy Pickard** and **Mike Hays** as keynote speakers. You can get a chance to talk to **Sue Hamilton,** publisher/editor. Law enforcement, including ex-G-man and author **Mark Bouton,** will be on hand just in case they are needed.

Swami says you're sure to learn a thing or two about crime writing and how to make it pay in seminars and conversations with people who've pulled off a scribbling job or two in their time. They will honor a local scribe, **Damon Runyon,** who took it on the lam some time back and became pals with guys to the wise in the other Manhattan.

It costs just a few potatoes to attend, and Swami swears it's better than twelve to seven that you'll come home a winner.

Marolyn Caldwell noticed the ad and asked if I could write a back story for a faux crime scene for a law enforcement panel to set up. I asked my friend Bob Iles to help. Working from a short story, "One Sweet Scam," that I wrote in the style of Damon Runyon, we set up a murder scenario for attendees to investigate, complete with an opening radio announcement at breakfast, clue sheets, physical evidence throughout the hotel, and an amazingly realistic scene of the crime. All was revealed at the final banquet when the "ghost" of the "murdered man" demanded an accounting. The three stories that follow all took place in Runyon's Manhattan.

One Sweet Scam

Manhattan, New York, 1938

I am sitting in Mindy's restaurant at about two in the morning, enjoying a cheesecake and watching Gentleman Johnny as he prepares to relieve a young man fresh to our fair city of his excess ducats. Johnny is known as a gentleman because he never takes a man's very last dollar and he always leaves the mark with a story he can tell. The less refined members of the city have been known to leave rubes with nothing more than a headache and an empty wallet. So the kid, named Eddie, is lucky that he is about to be taken to the cleaners by such an outstanding citizen as Johnny.

We patrons of this fine eating establishment are all in a good mood. At this time of the morning the dice are cooling, the ponies and the marks are safely tucked in for the night, and today's tout sheet hasn't hit the newsstands yet. A few of us are mentally adding up yesterday's take. The rest of us are certain that today Lady Luck will grab our arms and escort us followers of the sport of kings throughout the entire racing card.

Eddie looks like he combed the hay out of his hair just before he stepped through the door. He is regarding Johnny with a look he might have given back home in Kansas to a man who promised he could make it rain.

Says Johnny, taking the lid off the sugar bowl, "It is a simple matter of probabilities. I will put six cubes in a row on the table. Then we will both sit quietly and wait. I will bet that a fly will land on one specific cube. You will bet that a fly will land on any one of the other five. I have one chance in six. You have five chances out of six."

"How can you know which one a fly will land on?" asks the young man.

"They are big city flies," explains Johnny. "I have been around long enough to know how things operate in the big city. You have not."

Eddie says, "They look just like the flies back home to me."

"I will give you advice," says Johnny. "It is free. You should listen because it will help you get along here. Things are not always what they appear to be here in the big city."

"Thanks, I'll remember that," says Eddie.

"There is one thing...."

"I knew it," interrupts Eddie. "What's the catch?"

"There is no catch," answers the gentleman. "It's just that to lessen my disadvantage you put up two dollars for every one I risk. You put up a C note and I put up half as much."

The kid shakes his head. "I don't have that much. Besides, why should I give you odds? I know there's a trick to this. I just don't know what it is. I'll put up a double sawbuck. That's as much as I can stand to lose."

Johnny says, "I do not know if it is worth betting so little."
Of course the rest of us have been listening in.

Lefty Tucker speaks up. "Johnny, maybe you'd consider a little side action. I'll take your odds and lay out two C's."

Johnny says, "You're on. Anybody else want in?"

Pig Iron Murphy puts up half a G. Paulie the Pony adds five sawbucks. Even the professor drops a wrinkled fin into the well. Then everyone in the restaurant crowds around the table as Johnny places six white cubes in a row with about two inches between each of the cubes. They look identical to me.

Johnny asks the kid, "Which one do you think a fly will land on first?"

The kid stares at each one before pointing to one on the very end of the line.

Johnny shakes his head. "I'm putting my money on the one next to it. If the fly lands on any other cube, you win." Almost immediately a fly lands on Johnny's cube. In the hubbub that follows, I keep my eyes on the table. A waiter gathers up the cubes, drops them in the sugar bowl and whisks it off to the kitchen, leaving behind a few white grains on the table. I lick the tip of one finger, drag it over the grains and put it in my mouth.

Eddie antes up and shakes Johnny's hand. Big Louie blocks the door, and, one at a time, the other losers pay off with hardly any grumbling at all. It makes me proud to be associated with such classy mugs. Then an argument breaks out about how Johnny knew where the fly would land.

Pig Iron claims, "He trained those flies."

Paulie the Pony says, "He put a drop of whiskey on one sugar cube. Those were bar flies."

The professor pops his cork, "I don't understand. This flies in the face of reason."

Johnny lets the noise rise and then calls for attention: "Gentlemen, gentlemen. Our young friend stood up to the task and then paid his debt without complaint, unlike some of you pikers." Everybody laughs. "Being as he is still wet behind the ears, I say we give him the chance to get some money back. Now, I could lay this bet again at Harper's, Big Tony's and a dozen other hash houses as long as nobody knows how to pull it off. But I will let everyone here of the betting persuasion ante up a double sawbuck, which gets him one guess at how I knew which cube the fly would land on. If anybody gets it right, they split the pot with Eddie. If nobody gets it right, Eddie and I split the take. Those saps that don't bet can leave now and the rest will promise never to give away the answer. That is, if anybody guesses right."

Nobody answers for a minute but nobody heads for the exit, either. The professor clears his throat. "What if more than one person guesses right?"

"Then the pot will be divided between everyone who guesses right and Eddie."

Nobody wants to ask the question we all have. We all know that the gentleman is as honest as any mug in the city. But he has been known to ventilate a few guys when he had to with help from Mr. Smith and Mr. Wesson. A wise man stays on his good side.

To my surprise, it is the professor who asks it: "How do we know that, if we guess right, you will admit it?"

Johnny says, "I will tell Eddie how I knew which one to pick. He's a winner either way so it doesn't matter to him." Johnny whispers something in Eddie's ear. They pass around papers and pencils. Each man writes down his name and his guess, which takes time since some of us haven't filled out anything more complicated than a racing form for years.

I sit and noodle things out until the penny finally drops. Then I ease over to Eddie.

Quietly I say, "You've got one sweet scam."

"I've got? Don't you mean Johnny's got?"

I say, "Johnny's a fine gentleman, but he's not Santa Claus. He wouldn't give you half the pot unless he had to. You thought this up, not Johnny."

Eddie says, "You know how this works then? Write it down and you'll get half the loot."

I say, "I could do that or I could keep it to myself for half the loot later on and five percent of the take for as long as you run the scam. If nobody knows how you do it, you can keep it going longer. Think of it as another expense. Mindy knows everything that happens in his restaurant. You had to cut him in. And the waiter must be getting something for his part."

Eddie looks around and sees that the professor and Pig Iron are getting curious about our conversation. Others begin to notice. He lowers his voice.

"How did you figure it out?"

I say, "The waiter was too anxious to get the sugar bowl back to the kitchen. He didn't wipe the table off and I tasted what fell off the cubes. Next time you run it, be sure to tell the waiter to wipe the table."

A few of the men wander our way.

Eddie says in a whisper, "You can tell everybody how the scam works?"

I tell him. "It's right on the tip of my tongue."

He smiles at me and nods. We have a deal. I smile back, remembering how surprised I was by the taste of salt. With five cubes made of salt and only one made of sugar, it was no wonder

Murder Manhattan Style

Johnny could tell where the fly would land. I could tell that Eddie was going to go far.

Java Judy

Manhattan, New York, 1938

I am sitting in Mindy's Restaurant on Broadway at about two o'clock in the morning, engaged in a competition based on the knowledge of probabilities, experience with human nature and skill in prevarication. The contest goes by the moniker of Two Up and Three Down Five-Card Stud. A doll walks in who looks familiar. I puzzle my noodle until the penny drops. I check my hole card just to be sure. I'm right. The queen of hearts and the dame walking toward me could be sisters. This makes her one of the best-looking women to ever wear shoe leather.

She walks around looking at the cards. With the queen and jack of hearts kissing the table and the ten, nine and eight of hearts showing, I have the best hand. Of course, the other players don't know that. I might have a ten high, a straight or a flush. Lefty Tucker has the highest hand showing — three wise men. If he picks up the fourth king, he beats a straight and flush. Whatever he has, he loses to my straight flush. If we were playing with a deck of his cards, he would know that because he would know every card from marking the deck. That's why we never play with his cards.

Gentleman Johnny's Huey, Dewey and Louie are the next highest cards visible. The three twos look puny against light-fingered Tucker's kings, but Johnny's still in the pot. That means that all four of the twos might be residing in his hand. I would lay odds that Johnny, Lefty or both of them have Quads. Luckily for me, I have the nuts.

Pig Iron Murphy has a hockey stick and a Route 66 up. His best possible hand is a full house — sevens over sixes. Pig Iron is a master at using brass knuckles in dark alleys but figuring odds is not his forte. I make a mental note not to leave the restaurant alone. The ruffian sitting next to me has been known to get his table stakes back by sapping the sap that won them.

The newest addition to our fellowship of fortune seekers, Sweet Eddie, tossed in his hand when the first pair popped up. Seeing what happened since then proves what a good decision he made. To win at poker, you want to limit your losses but not your winnings. He did one; I am about to do the other.

The woman smiles at Eddie and asks, "Are you ready for our date?"

"I'm arranging financing right now," says Eddie. "Gents, I'd like you to meet Java Judy."

We trade introductions. She glances at his stash. "This could take a while. You'll need a lot more than that to take me out. Do you gentlemen mind if I sit and watch?" None of us mind perusing eye candy, even if she has a date with young Eddie, so we ask for a chair. She sits between Lefty and me, directly across from her intended swain.

I make a small bet. Murphy calls. Johnny makes a big raise. Tucker doubles that. Everybody stays in, although Murphy is starting to sweat. It's back to me for the last time. I double Tucker's bet.

When Murphy raises his eyebrows and looks at me, I say, "I've got you beat. Save your money." He folds.

Java Judy

Johnny asks, "Do you have me beat, too?"

"Why else would I bet?" I ask.

He folds.

Tucker is practically drooling on his kings. "Can I see your cards?"

"Sure," I say. "Just call the bet and I'll flip them right over."

Tucker drums his fingers on the table. "You're not going to tell me to save my money?"

"It probably hasn't been yours very long," I say. "You just can't keep your hands out of somebody else's hip pocket."

"It's mine now," says Tucker. He pulls a wallet out of his pocket, opens it and looks at the driver's license before asking, "Who is Damon Runyon, anyway?"

None of us know. Tucker tosses in a wad of green. He turns over the fourth king and a seven. I smile and flip over the winning cards.

As I rake in the loot, Judy slides her chair closer to me. "You're got nearly enough to take me out, even with my expensive tastes." She smiles in Eddie's direction. "I usually leave with the winner."

"Then you won't leave with that guy," says Eddie. "He plays every night, but he's never the biggest winner."

I explain. "He's right. Sometimes I win. Sometimes I lose. Somebody else always walks away with bigger pots."

Judy smiles. "Tonight might be different." She pats me on the arm before leaving the table. I slow play the next few hands, breaking even as the deal passes around the table with each hand. I smell coffee and look over my shoulder. Carrying a cup of java, Judy sits down right next to me. She sets the cup down in front of the deck. I deal right over it.

Murder Manhattan Style

"You like black coffee," I say.

"Straight and strong," she says, "just the way I like my men."

I read my hole cards and dump them, losing my ante. Tucker deals the next hand. While we play, Judy keeps her cup full. I make a little bit when others deal. I win a lot when it's my turn.

"She brings you luck," says the gentleman.

"I couldn't do it without her," I agree.

In an hour and a half, I have so many silver certificates and Federal Reserve notes in my hoard that I could open a bank. The jousting concludes for the night. Eddie walks out, looking back over his shoulder at Judy. She ignores him and stays with me.

"Eddie's a nice kid," Judy says after he leaves. "I didn't want to break his heart by going out with him until he ran out of money and then kicking him to the curb so I could be with a man with deeper pockets."

"Is that why you helped me?" I ask.

She nods.

I say, "I never realized that coffee would reflect the cards dealt over it."

"Only black coffee," says Judy. " A magician showed me. When Eddie told me you were never the biggest winner, I knew that you play cards for money instead of bragging rights. You let the players focus on somebody else every time, not noticing how much you walk away with."

"You helped me win this money. You should help me spend it. What happens after it's gone?" I look at her quizzically and ask, "Are you going to break my heart?"

She tilts her head and looks back at me. She takes my arm. We head toward the door before she answers: "Buy me a cup of

Java Judy

java and we'll see what happens."

Author's note: I think this fluffy little story will always be special to me. I have multiple myeloma (bone marrow cancer). I got a bone marrow transplant in January 2008. I had a very good partial remission instead of the lousy total remission I was hoping for. At my current level of cancer, I am totally off chemotherapy. As long as it stays at the current level, I won't need treatment. For some months after I got home, I could not concentrate long enough to read a novel. As I gradually recovered, I became able to read with attention. Next I was able to edit work I'd done before. Eventually I was able to write out a story I had fully developed in my head long before. Finally I was able to take an idea all the way from conception to finished story. You just read it.

A Detective's Romance

A scream like a banshee's wail echoed through the hallway, wobbling the pane of glass in the office door and the letters painted on it that spelled out "Richard Ellis, Private Investigator — Reliable and Discreet." Smaller print at the bottom read, "Walk In."

Inside, Stephanie, pouring coffee into a mug Ellis held in his clenched fist, did not flinch. Ellis opened his bloodshot eyes and muttered, "I don't know why she doesn't just say 'hello' like everybody else."

"Because it's what everybody else does," answered Stephanie. "What fun would that be?"

"Why is the sun so bright at the crack of dawn?" Ellis complained.

"It's eight thirty and overcast," answered Stephanie.

The door flew open and a woman flounced in — Mary Beth Jackson, self-styled pride of Atlanta, dressed to impress. She had the self-assurance to pull it off. A close look might reveal that she was a few years past the age to play the elusive ingénue roles she stalked on and off Broadway. Her body had ripened just a bit more than fashion preferred. But her tailored winter coat enhanced her still striking figure and her wide-

Murder Manhattan Style

brimmed hat set off her innocent-looking blue eyes.

"Sorry about the rebel yell, ya'll," Mary Beth said. "I thought I spotted some Yankees before I remembered I was in New York. Nearly everybody here is a Yankee. Of course I'm not talking about Lou Gehrig, Joe DiMaggio and their lot."

"Mary Beth, you could write for Jack Benny's radio show," said Stephanie, laughing.

Mary Beth shook her head. "There are too many Yankees in Hollywood."

"Is that coffee?" Mary Beth snatched the mug from under Ellis's nose and drank it down while Ellis groped for the handle.

"This stuff will stunt your growth," she cooed to Ellis. "You really don't want any."

Stephanie and Mary Beth levered Ellis to a standing position and stepped back. He swayed but did not fall.

"The camera is on the desk," said Stephanie. "Why don't you grab it while I get the great detective into his overcoat?"

"Can you manage it alone?"

"Easily. He's not drunk — just hung over," said Stephanie.

Mary Beth picked up the camera and left her purse on the desk. She led Ellis out of his office. "Come on, honey. It's mid-February and payday for us. We're playing 'Love in New York.' Remember? I explained it to you yesterday. You stay in the background and look menacing when I give you the cue. I have the opening lines."

They returned at eight that evening. Ellis shoved a gigantic bouquet of flowers at Stephanie.

"Oh, thank you," said Stephanie. "Who were these for?" She fished a note out of the bouquet and read it. "These were for Gertrude. I hope poor Gertrude didn't get her feelings crushed."

"Poor Gertrude has a better fastball than Lefty Gomez,"

70

said Ellis. "She's not afraid to throw inside high and hard. As soon as Mary Beth started her patter, Gertrude threw these in my face and started cursing like a sailor coming off shore leave. She wasn't crushed."

Ellis blew on his hands and rubbed them together. "It was cold out there."

"Fiddlesticks," said Mary Beth. "Fresh air is good for you." She picked up her purse and took out a cigarette. She lit it and inhaled deeply. Then she blew a smoke ring in the shape of a heart.

"How did it go?" asked Stephanie.

"It was the highest-paying role I've had all year," said Mary Beth. "I love playing the lead. I don't know why I didn't come up with the idea sooner. I just wish we could pull it off more than one day a year."

Mary Beth pirouetted, tilted her head and winked at Stephanie.

"We approach couples out spooning and take their pictures before they know what's happening. We tell them we are doing a photo spread on love in the big city that we hope to sell to *Life* or *Look*. After that, it's up to them how to respond."

"It still seems like a lousy thing to do to someone on Valentine's Day," said Stephanie, raising her eyebrows.

"That's not so," said Ellis. "Some nice couples just smiled and wished us good luck. Others offered to pay for a print once we get the film developed. We got their names and addresses plus we collected five dollars each time. We'll get the photos developed and send them off as promised. They get a nice memento and we make more than enough to cover expenses."

Ellis took out a small roll of bills and put it on the desk.

"I have to admit we made more money this time from cou-

Murder Manhattan Style

ples who wanted to be sure that there weren't any photos of them," said Mary Beth.

She took out a much larger role of bills and dropped it on the desk next to the smaller pile.

"The great detective had to discourage a few lugs from breaking the camera."

"That cost them extra," said Ellis. "I suppose one or two of the girls were shocked to find out how badly their lover boys didn't want the world to know about their romances. It wasn't *us* being mean. It gave the girls a chance to wise up."

"We split it like we agreed? Sixty-forty?" Mary Beth asked Stephanie.

"Oh no, dear," answered Stephanie, smiling. "You deserve half of the profits. After all, it was your idea. You knew you couldn't pull it off by yourself. Neither could Ellis. You also knew that a lot of men would go along with your plan until the end of the day and then keep all the money. Ellis wouldn't do that." She counted the money while Mary Beth and Ellis talked.

"I won't have to sling hash for a while," said Mary Beth. "I can go to auditions whenever they're held. I hear there's a casting call for 'A Slight Case of Murder'."

"Good luck," said Ellis.

"Thanks," said Mary Beth. She motioned Ellis into the hall, closing the door behind them.

"Tell me, Ellis. Why did you buy flowers for Stephanie and then put another woman's name on the card?"

"She deserves flowers for putting up with me all year," said Ellis. "It wouldn't be much of a gift if I gave her flowers some tootsie threw at us."

"But that's what she thinks you did," said Mary Beth.

"If I put my name on the card, she might get the wrong

idea."

"You mean she might think you actually care about her?" asked Mary Beth.

Ellis grimaced. "She's a nice kid. She deserves better than a broken down ex-cop. If I gave her flowers and asked her out, eventually it wouldn't work out. When she dumped me, she'd quit. I'd lose the best secretary I ever had. This way she gets to enjoy the flowers and she still gets to act cynical about it."

Mary Beth shook her head. "You survived the depression and the mean streets of New York but you're scared to tell Stephanie you're carrying a torch for her. You're a bigger chump than the men we just fleeced."

Author's note: Sometimes people ask where ideas for stories came from. The premise of this story came from a newspaper article I read on Valentine's Day a few years ago. I was surprised to learn that the holiday was the busiest day of the year for private detectives. Apparently, it's a great day to catch people who cheat on their spouses and/or lovers.

.

Author's note: My friend, Bob Isles, announced publication of his last novel at the Great Manhattan Mystery Conclave III. He has passed away since then and I miss him. Bob offered feedback about my writing that helped make me a much better writer. He was also kind enough to allow me to use the Manhattan setting of his character, Peter B. Bruck, for a short story of my own. The three stories that follow all take place in what I like to think of as Bob Isles' post-World War II New York.

The Wrong Man

Manhattan, New York, 1947

The bulls shoved me through the precinct doors and double-timed me down the hall into the interrogation room. They pushed me down onto a stool and turned a bright light toward my face so I couldn't see a thing. Somebody standing close behind me slapped a nightstick into his palm.

"All you can get me for is sitting down on the job," I said. "That's no crime. Not with what they pay me."

Nobody answered.

"Turn that light off. I'm a veteran. I pay your salaries."

"You're breaking my heart. So sing like Frankie Lane," the voice came from the darkness.

"This runt would sound more like one of the Andrews Sisters," said another voice.

While they laughed, I thought back to how I got into this.

75

Murder Manhattan Style

I was sitting behind the desk in the office of Peter B. Bruck, Private Investigator. It was about six-thirty in the evening. A man's voice on the radio assured me, "The rest of 1947 will be just like a slice of heaven." I switched him off. Dedicated drones in other offices still labored away, but of course Bruck was long gone. I was supposed to be sweeping the floor and emptying the trash. Instead, I was taking advantage of Bruck's absence to peruse a magazine that he and I both enjoy for its literary humor and appreciation of the human form. Some janitors like to wear a uniform all the time. I, on the other hand, prefer to do my heavy work in janitor's garb late at night and to dress like a banker the rest of time. It's a free country, after all. I know. I fought to keep it that way.

The door opened. She sashayed in. Tall and brunette, she could have stepped off a pin-up poster. She wore a little red scarf. The top three buttons of her white blouse were unbuttoned and her dark blue skirt was wartime short. I so admire patriotic women.

"I'm Roxie Terry. You've got to help me," she pleaded. "You're my only hope. The cops can't do anything."

How could I have dashed her hopes and told her that Bruck was probably off in some bar getting hammered and spending money he owes for alimony? I slipped the magazine into a desk drawer.

"Why don't you enlighten me?" I asked. "I've been able to clean up some real messes in my day. I might be able to help you."

"What do you charge?" she asked.

I quoted her Bruck's fees for the services he is willing to admit he performs.

Roxie listened and then shook her head. "That doesn't

cover what I need."

She sat in a chair and crossed her legs. She had my full attention. She leaned forward. I didn't think it was possible, but my attention got even fuller.

"Men take advantage of my loving nature," she sighed.

"Imagine that," I said. I did and almost lost track of what she was saying.

"When I love a man, I really love him. One of my former boyfriends took advantage of my trust. He took photos of me really loving him. Now I have a chance with a swell guy. He's a dentist. My old boyfriend is threatening to show him the photos. My new boyfriend won't want me after that."

"He might want you more."

"No," she said smiling, "some men would – the slugs – but my new boyfriend is a real square. He's a Rotarian. He said he'll marry me in a heartbeat and take me back to meet his family in Iowa. That's just what a girl like me wants, but I keep putting him off because of the pictures."

"So you want someone to get the photos for you."

She nodded.

I thought about it.

"Photos can be copied," I said. "Even if someone got them for you, there might be another set around."

"My old boyfriend wouldn't allow that to happen. He wants to keep them to himself, just like he wants to keep me to himself. He developed the photos himself. He keeps the originals and negatives in his private office and he refuses to give them to me."

"Who is your old boyfriend?"

"Frank Arcona."

I whistled. Frank "Kodak" Arcona had his own darkroom.

Murder Manhattan Style

He also had a dark reputation as a loan shark, gambler and political fixer with ties to the mob. Frank was rumored to have a private collection of photos of people who failed to repay their loans in a timely manner, which, by themselves, strongly encouraged fiscal responsibility. I knew he had a place that looked like a bank and was crawling with arm twisters and leg breakers. I drummed my fingers on the desk, wondering what Boston Blackie or Sam Spade would have done. If the radio programs needed an idea for a script, I had a doozy for them.

"Did you tell anybody you were coming here?"

"No."

"You're certain?"

"Yes."

I spoke slowly, thinking out loud: "*If* I can get the pictures for you, Arcona will know they're gone. He'll guess you were involved, but he won't know who helped you. I don't want his collectors working me over. I can't promise anything, but I'll try. I'll need an advance for expenses and a week's pay to see if it can be done."

"I'll write you a check."

"No, that would leave a trace back to me. Arcona could squeeze the information from somebody at your bank. I need cash and the name and phone number of someone you trust absolutely. If I can get the pictures, I'll call that person. He or she will call you with a date and time to get together. I'll meet you in the Chinese restaurant down the street exactly twenty-four hours before the scheduled date and time. Come alone and bring more cash. Be ready to leave town immediately without telling anybody. Tell your fiancé to be ready to leave at a moment's notice without saying a word to anybody. If I have the pictures, I'll bring them along."

The Wrong Man

She bit her lip.

"How long will it take?"

"Give me six weeks. I need to see if it can be done and I'll need time to set it up. If you don't hear from me by then, I couldn't pull it off. Don't come back here for any reason. If you decide to go to the cops, Lieutenant Thompson from this precinct is an honest guy – for a cop."

Roxie nodded.

"Tell me how many pictures there are and exactly what I'm looking for. I don't want to risk going in twice."

I don't think I blushed.

Within three days I was in Arcona's office. He was tough. He was smart. He hired loyal mugs. But he didn't mop his own floor. I brought along a Leica camera I had picked up from a soldier who had no more use for it, just in case. Like everyone else who owned a safe, Arcona kept the combination close by. In less than ten minutes I found it taped to the bottom of the phone. I found lots of photos and negatives in Arcona's safe. Roxie had an unusually loving nature with a wide range of partners. The shots of her with the mayor might have helped his re-election campaign, but the shots of her with the mayor's wife probably would not. With a little work I was able to replace the first few negatives and photos with similar materials that did not include Roxie. I thought it might stand up to a brief glance and buy Roxie a little time.

I called Roxie's friend and met with Roxie in the restaurant. She promised to leave for Iowa with her Rotarian dentist that night. I gave her the negatives and the pictures. She was relieved when I swore she had all the originals. She took scissors out of her purse, cut them into tiny strips and left them in the

79

trash. Of course she didn't ask if I'd made copies. I think I mentioned before that I'm an admirer of human aesthetics.

The other photos in Arcona's safe bothered me. There were photos of men brutally beaten and maimed. There even a few photos of dead men, probably suicides. Dead men rarely pay their debts. For a few weeks I kept the janitor's job at Arcona's place. Then this morning the cops rousted me out of my comfortable bed and dragged here me into the interrogation room. Somebody shut off the light in my face when Lieutenant Thompson walked into the room.

"Are you ready to talk, hero?" asked Thompson. "You boys can knock off the tough stuff with this one. I don't care if he looks like Mickey Rooney; he acts like John Wayne. After what he went through in the war, you boys can't scare him, and believe me, you don't want to make him mad."

"If you're supposed to be the good cop," I said, "you need to work on your act. What's all this about?"

"We got us a real hero here," said Thompson. "He's got the scars and the medals to prove it. It's just that for the rest of us the war is over, but not for him. We found Frank Arcona at the bottom of a fire escape this morning. His neck was snapped."

"Falls can do that," I answered.

"So can you. There was soap scum on the floor of his office, the top rungs of the fire escape, and the soles of Arcona's shoes."

"Sounds like he was careless. It's a dangerous world."

"Especially with you around," said Thompson. "Arcona's wall safe was open, but it only had girlie pictures in it. There was no ledger of debts, none of his famous pictures, no cash and no guns."

Thompson lit a cigarette. "I know what happened. He surprised you in his office going through his safe. So you broke his neck. Then you made it look like he caught a burglar rifling his safe and tried to chase him down the fire escape. You tossed him out of the window."

"You ought to write for the radio, Lieutenant. You have a wonderful imagination. If somebody did that, it wasn't me. You've got the wrong man."

I looked Thompson straight in the eye as I said it. It was true. My feelings were a little bit hurt that Thompson would suspect me of doing that. Surprised me in his office, indeed. Thompson had no idea how hard it was to get Arcona to come into the office late at night and alone.

Authors note: I wrote this story initially for a magazine asking for submissions that included elements from radio detective programs of the 1940s and 1950s. I had fun writing about a protagonist who took over the story and pushed it in a direction I had not anticipated. Then the market went out of business, which happens all too often. Personally, I thought that was an overreaction. Lots of places reject my stories and manage to stay in business. Anyway, I was left with an unusual orphaned story that did not fit the usual mold for short stories.

I submitted it to a number of markets and each time I collected a rejection with positive comments from editors. It's encouraging to get feedback. Anyone who takes the time to comment on a rejected story is giving the submitting author a gift. The great majority of rejections I get are just standard postcards or rejection letters. This story holds the record among my stories for getting the most rejections along with the most positive editorial comments. I was sufficiently encouraged to keep

Murder Manhattan Style

sending it out, hoping it would find a home somewhere. In the end I was able to find more than one market for this. This is my favorite story to read aloud at book signings.

Funeral Games

Manhattan, New York, 1948

Dead bodies don't look like they were ever living, breathing people. Even intact bodies, like those floating off Omaha Beach or frozen to the ground in the Ardennes forest, look less than human. Emaciated bodies stacked like firewood in a concentration camp look like a nightmare of hell worse than any paining by Hieronymus Bosch. They don't look human. I don't sleep much because every time I close my eyes, I see dead bodies.

The body lying in my brother's mahogany casket resembled Denny, but it looked more like a wax museum figure. Its face was an unnatural shade of pink.

"Excuse me," said a man, putting his hand on my shoulder. "We need to talk."

I repressed the urge to slug him for touching me. I don't like to be touched. I looked up at him. He was matinee-idol-handsome with black hair and a thin moustache. His well-tailored suit made his broad shoulders look even wider than they actually were and only hinted at the shoulder holster underneath. I knew who he was. Behind him was an even bigger and younger man with auburn hair, who I also recognized.

"Let me buy you a cup of coffee," the man suggested.

Murder Manhattan Style

I looked over at Denny's widow, Janie. Blond and statuesque, she looked lovely and vulnerable in black. I didn't want her to get upset so I allowed myself to be steered out of the funeral home to a nearby café. The man chose a table with a view out the side window in the back of the busy café. He sat with his back to the wall. The other man sat facing the window. I faced them.

"Do you know who I am?" the handsome man asked.

I'd seen his picture in the paper. Duke Palermo was a mobster. Bluebloods liked to have their pictures taken with him to impress their friends. He ran one of the bright lights on Broadway where you could satisfy any desire the deepest, darkest part of your psyche could dream up. Gambling, pornography, drugs, loans impossible to repay, prostitution with any gender and age – whatever your poison, Palermo would sell it to you.

"No, but I recognize Dynamite Malone." I turned to the younger man. "I saw you beat Terry Brown. I don't care what the official outcome was. The ref must have been paid off to give a long count to Brown in the third round and a short count to you in the sixth."

"I slipped," said Malone. "He missed me with an upper cut. I got tangled up in the ropes. The damn ref had to skip some numbers fast as he counted."

Palermo gritted his teeth.

"I thought he tagged you," I answered. "The ref started counting before you hit the canvas."

Malone said, "Maybe Brown tapped me, but I slipped."

Palermo cut in, "We didn't come here to discuss ancient history. We got business. My name is Duke Palermo. You might have heard of me."

He looked at me expectantly.

I shook my head no and looked over at Malone again.

"You beat Alfie Gonzales, too. You knocked him all around the ring for the whole fight. I know you didn't put him down, but he has a head like a bowling ball. He's never been knocked down. The judges must have been on the take."

Malone said, "You're right."

Palermo struck like a snake, backhanding Malone and leaving a red mark.

"I warned you," snarled Palermo. "When I want to talk business, you keep your trap shut and watch out for trouble. You don't listen to the business. If some mug tries to talk to you, you ignore him. Now sit there like the dummy you are."

"You didn't need to do that," I said to Palermo.

"He never was an Einstein," said Palermo. "He took too many punches and now he's washed up in the fight game. He hasn't got the brains for honest work and I'm sap enough to give him a job. But let's get down to business. I run a club on Broadway. I'm sorry about your brother. Everybody knows how he dodged Jap Zeros, became an ace and came home without a scratch. A year later, a stolen taxi flattens him. It's one thing to survive World War II. Staying alive these days in New York City is something else."

"Ironic," I replied.

"Did they ever find the driver?"

"No."

Palermo leaned toward me. "The thing is, your brother never got over the war. He needed excitement to feel alive."

"That's not me. I just want to be left alone."

"He gambled at my place. Sometimes he won big. Other times he lost a bundle. He didn't seem to care. I let it ride. It was good for business to have a big war hero in my joint. He added class and attracted the swells. Just before he died, your brother ran into a long losing streak. He was into me for five thousand dollars."

"I can give you the name of the attorney handling his estate, but I don't think he had much money."

"No shyster is going take a marker. Now that Denny's dead, he can't pay off the marker. My boss wants to know where that money will come from."

I nodded and sipped my coffee.

"In his memory, you could repay your brother's debt," said Palermo.

"It's not my debt," I answered. "In his memory, I could see that my sister-in-law is looked out for."

"I've met her," said Palermo. "I have to tell you, if you can't pay back your brother's debt, I wouldn't mind collecting it from her, one night at a time."

I dropped my hands to the chair and gripped hard to keep from smashing my fists into Palermo's face.

"I don't understand," I said. "Five thousand dollars is a lot to me. I'm a janitor. To you it's just pocket change. And I thought you mob guys left families of civilians alone."

Palermo said, "Okay, I'll level with you. You're right. I take in more than five grand in profit on a good Saturday night and my boss wouldn't like it if I messed with your brother's widow. But I won't let it slide."

Palermo poked his finger into my chest. I had an urge to kick him in the nuts. "Your brother got under my skin. He acted like he was better than me. What did he have that I don't? He was a war hero, but I've been fighting all my life. I fought my way up out of the gutter. They don't hand out medals for that. The swells come to my place because it's the popular thing to do right now. Next week or next month they'll get bored and find a new thrill. I'll go back to being a bum in their eyes. But your brother could do no wrong. Rich guys, the mayor, maybe even the president would be happy to talk to him. He ran up a debt and he didn't worry about paying it back. He wasn't even scared of me."

Palermo's eyes bored into me. "You're just like him. I won't let him end up getting something over on me. One way or another, I will get even."

I sighed, realizing that he wasn't going to give it up. "Give me a few days," I said. "Maybe I can come up with something."

"I know about you, too," said Palermo. "Another war hero."

Malone turned his head toward me. Palermo didn't notice.

"No," I said, "the real heroes didn't make it home. About my brother, though, he was better than you."

Palermo whipped out his pistol and pointed it between my eyes. The noise in the café diminished and then stopped. People stared at us.

"Are you going to shoot me?" I asked. "In front of all these witnesses? Go ahead. The mob would disown you for sheer stupidity. As pretty as you are, I bet in the prison shower room you'd always have your dance card full." I raised my voice and said, "The man with the gun is Duke Palermo. Remember and be ready to testify about it. Duke Palermo."

Palermo's hand shook. Slowly he returned the pistol to his holster.

"I'll see you later," hissed Palermo. He stood up and walked out of the café without a backward glance. Malone gave me a worried look and hurried after him.

Lieutenant Randall looked me up late that night while I

mopped the floor of the hallway outside the offices in the Acme Building.

"I heard about what happened," said Randall. "Palermo isn't as nuts as Bugsy Siegel, but he's dangerous. You might want to skip town for a while."

"Thanks for the advice, Lieutenant, but if I disappear he'll go after my sister-in-law, Janie. For her to be safe, I need him to focus on me."

"Luciano and Laskey won't like that he's bothering civilian family members, especially family members of a war hero," said Randall.

"You must know somebody who could clue them in."

"They won't do anything about it," warned Randall. "Palermo brings the rich in and he makes a mint for the mob. He's got a rotten temper. Someday he'll tromp on the wrong set of toes and get a visit from Murder Incorporated, but it won't be soon."

"I know, but it might help to get the word out."

"Anything else I can do for you?"

"Yes. Pull back the men you've got watching me and keep them far away from for a while. Captain O'Bannon is going to find out that you've got men on a stakeout when no crime has been committed. He'll be after your scalp. Even if they saw Palermo enter the building, what could they do?"

Randall frowned, but he nodded. "I talked to the detectives working on your brother's death and told them a snitch said it was murder. They're going to treat it that way from now on. One of the witnesses said the taxi waited until your brother was in the middle of the street before it ran the red light. We discounted her testimony at the time since nobody else saw it that way. I was never satisfied that we knew why the taxi was stolen and then just abandoned."

"Thanks, I appreciate it."

I kept mopping. It wasn't long after he left that I heard Dynamite Malone doing a bad impression of a cat burglar. I walked up behind him and let the mop handle fall to the floor. Malone nearly jumped out of his skin.

"Were you looking for me?"

"You scared me out of ten years' growth," said Malone.

"Good. You're big enough already."

"You gotta get out of here. Palermo's coming and he's loaded for bear. I told him I'd come in first and soften you up for him, but he won't wait long."

"I know."

"I was too young to get into the war, but I appreciate what you and your brother did. I wanted to warn you about Palermo. You embarrassed him in the restaurant. He hates being shown up. He used to hate your brother especially. I don't know why."

"The same reason he hates you," I said. I reached up and touched his chin with my fingers, moving his face from side to side to look at the bruises.

"He's been using you for a punching bag, hasn't he? My brother was real. You were a real contender. That's why he had my brother killed and why he ruined your boxing career. He's not a real man. He gets nervous and angry when he runs into one."

Malone looked puzzled. "How did you know he was the one who ruined my career?"

"The night before you fought Gonzales, did a woman come to your room and wear you out all night long?"

"How did you know that?"

"Put it together, Malone. Who made money when you lost

those two bouts? A gambler. Who could fix a referee and judges? A mobster. Who could send you a woman to break your concentration and wear you out? A pimp. Who do you know that's a gambler, a mobster and a pimp who enjoys whacking you around and making fun of you?"

"I didn't do nothing to him," protested Malone.

"Neither did my brother, but Palermo had him killed. Neither did I, but when I didn't break out bawling after he pulled a gun, Palermo went ape, didn't he?"

Malone nodded. "He said he'd kill you."

"I've spent the last couple of years getting shot at," I answered. "I'm still standing. Thanks for the warning. Now get out of here. You're a good kid. You shouldn't be hanging around with scum like Palermo."

"I'll leave if you do."

I shook my head. "He'd go after my sister-in-law, Janie, then. I have to stay and see it through. You need to get out."

"Yeah, get the hell out of my sight." Palermo stormed toward us. "Softening him up, dummy? After I finish off this jerk, I'm coming after you."

Palermo raised a fist to Malone. Malone chopped a short left into Palermo's ribs and knocked him into the wall. Palermo's head bounced off the wall and he staggered. Malone smashed Palermo's nose with a right cross. Palermo slammed into the wall again. His legs went out from under him and he slid down into a sitting position.

Palermo pulled his pistol and started firing. The first shot went wild. The second shot grazed Malone's skull, leaving a long red welt just above his ear. Malone collapsed. Breathing heavily, Palermo stood up and took an unsteady step so he was standing over Malone. His hands shook as he fired all the bullets in the gun at Malone's fallen body. Then Palermo pulled the trigger four times more, not noticing that the weapon was empty.

I moved quickly over to Malone and knelt by him. He was leaking blood, but he was still breathing.

"That son of a bitch was trying to kill me," whined Palermo.

"He did kill you," I said. "He kept knocking your head against the wall until your brains were like scrambled eggs."

Palermo looked confused. "When did he do that?"

"Right now," I said, rising. I reached for the mop to unscrew the handle.

A few minutes later, Malone groaned and opened his eyes. "God, that hurts," he said.

"Take it easy, kid. The ambulance is on its way."

"What about Palermo?"

I glanced at Palermo's crumpled remains.

"He won't need one. You got up off the canvas and finished him. That's why they call you dynamite. When somebody hurts you, it just lights your fuse."

"Gee, I'm sorry I missed it."

"It wasn't much of a fight, really. A pretender can't do much against a real contender."

"Did I use my jab?"

"Yes. You kept him at arm's length with the jab. When he got close, you used the straight left and the right cross. He never laid a hand on you. You should have done that with Gonzales."

"Everybody tells me that. Do you think I could get a rematch?"

"Sure thing, kid. You can get another shot at Brown, too. You got a lot of heart. That will take you a long way."

Malone shuddered and grabbed my hand.

"I'm cold. Don't leave me alone. I'm scared."

"I'll stay with you as long as you want." I held his hand. The light went out of his eyes just before I heard the wail of the sirens in the distance. Lying in a heap, Malone's body didn't look like it had ever belonged to a human being.

Captain O'Bannon was mad that the building had been under surveillance and mad that the surveillance had been withdrawn. He questioned me himself, even though he was obviously out of practice.

"Tell me the story," he commanded.

He sounded like a spoiled brat demanding a bedtime story so I obliged him with a fairy tale. I told him that I heard shouts and noises. Then I heard the shots. Being the cautious type, I waited a long time before I investigated. When I saw the men, I went to them to see if they were alive. One was still living, so I called the ambulance. Then I went back to see if I could do anything. I was upset and I didn't remember how many times I walked through the blood or what I touched.

How did a man being beaten to death pull a trigger? How did a man dying of gunshot wounds beat another man to death? Not being there, I didn't know. Why were Palermo's wallet and pockets empty except for two lead pennies? I didn't know. Did the Captain know how much money Palermo usually carried? I didn't. The Captain backed off that line of questioning immediately. He kept after me and after me, but he wasn't very good.

I knew the men. One was a boxer and the other pulled a gun on me earlier in the day when he tried to get me to pay my dead brother's gambling debt, but there was nothing to connect me with the crime. I had blood on my hands and clothes, of course. I had touched the men to see if they were alive. The ambulance attendants found me still holding Malone's hand. I had no bruises on my body. My knuckles were not scraped or swollen. Then I told the Captain the truth for a change: I didn't punch Palermo and I didn't shoot Malone. Although he hated to do it, O'Bannon had to let me go the next morning. One good thing about the Captain having done the interview was that he could not blame Randall for the lack of results. I went home and slept for twenty-four hours.

Palermo's death was a three-day journalistic wonder. Some papers eulogized Palermo. Others declared Malone to be the hero. Some hinted darkly at conspiracies and unexplained mysteries. O'Bannon promised a clear solution to the puzzle, which, of course, he never delivered. I read all the papers. None of them mentioned me by name. One or two hinted there was a witness. The police refused to comment. One enterprising editor hired a lip reader who claimed O'Bannon muttered something about a "damn mob jockey" after one news conference. That set off a brief storm of speculation about fixed horse races. Nobody ever thought about a mop jockey.

When the police released the crime scene, I was the one who cleaned it up. Somehow it's always left to me to clean up the messes. When I was done, the floor and the wall were spotless. Just to be sure, I used nearly half a gallon of bleach cleaning the mop handle over and over again. Then I threw it in the garbage bin and got a new one. The handle had served me well, but you can't get sentimental about the tools of your trade.

I got a call from Janie a few weeks later. I arranged to meet her in the lobby of the Acme Building at dusk.

"You're really all right?" she asked. "Is this where it happened?"

"I'm fine," I said. "It happened in this building, but not right here."

"I've been doing a lot of thinking," she said. "I loved Denny. I don't know if I'll ever love another man as much. But he's dead and I have to think about my future." She bit her lip. "I don't suppose you've thought about us."

I had, of course. I often dreamed about having sex with her and every time I woke up shivering, with a pounding headache. That is another reason I don't sleep much. Why was I still alive when so many men were dead? I didn't deserve to even touch her. I fought down the desire to rip her clothes off and fuck her right then on the floor.

"I have thought about us," I said. "I love you. How could I not love the woman who was my brother's wife? I'll always love you and to me you'll always be Denny's wife."

"That's what I thought. I'm glad you came into some money recently. I won't accept your five thousand dollars. I don't believe Denny ever loaned you that much. He might have borrowed it from you, but he never would have saved that much money."

"Probably not," I admitted.

"You know that before I met Denny I was a ...."

"...party girl," I finished for her.

"That's a nice way to put it," she said. She smiled. "You've always been nice to me. I'm not going to become a kindergarten teacher now. I'm going to get a job in a nightclub. I can sing and dance a little. Maybe if I work in a place like Palermo used to run, I'll meet some society swell who'll want to take care of me. Palermo used to check me out every time I went into his place with Denny. I didn't mind. It made me feel good. I flirted a little but was never unfaithful to Denny." She paused. "Are you disappointed?"

"No," I said. "I know how you felt about Denny. What

Funeral Games

happened was not your fault. As to what you want to do, it's a free country. I know. I fought to keep it that way. If that's what you really want, do it."

I watched her walk away. For a little while I could see her when she walked under streetlights and when headlights from passing cars illuminated her. She got smaller and harder to see. Then she disappeared into the darkness.

Author's Note: After writing too many upbeat, hopeful stories, I find that I need to clear my head by writing something bleaker. I think noir literature goes back at least to ancient Greece if not even farther. The Iliad and The Odyssey include grimly realistic passages about war and suffering. In The Iliad, after a Greek hero's death, he was honored by other warriors with wrestling and racing contests called funeral games. Some readers prefer a darker type of fiction such as this.

The Turkey Hill Affair

Between the two Manhattans, 1948

Turkey Hill, Iowa, was a big disappointment until I bumped into Bennie as he was robbing the Farm and Business Bank. I was daydreaming, looking out the front window at a cute farmer boy walking by. So, when I say I bumped into Bennie, I mean I actually collided with him.

He dropped his gun and a sack stuffed with money. He reached for one and then for the other. When he saw me, he stopped and stared. Ever since I was fourteen I've had that effect on men. And Bennie, the big lug, has never been the sharpest pencil in the box.

I could see that Pop Thomas, the bank guard, was looking back and forth between Bennie and the ancient pistol on his own hip that he had lugged across the muddy battlefields of France during the First World War. I knew I would have to take charge or somebody was going to get damaged.

"No, don't hurt me," I yelled. I scooped up the gun and handed it to Bennie. Then I retrieved the bag of money and handed it over, too. I shouted, "Don't make me go with you," as I pushed Bennie toward the door. Luckily, Bennie was used to doing what other people told him to do.

I spoke to him softly, "Meet me outside the bank at ten

tonight, Bennie."

"Won't people see us, Roxie? Is that safe?"

"This isn't New York. They roll up the sidewalk at eight. Now shove me away and get out of town."

Bennie gave me a little push. I managed to twist around and grab the bank guard in a hard embrace. I started sobbing. "Don't let him hurt me." I pulled Pop Thomas's head to my chest. Thomas hugged me back. His body responded to my closeness. Who would have thought there was so much life left in the old codger? When the sheriff arrived a few minutes later, he had to practically pry us apart.

Sheriff Allen was a dreamboat redhead with a wide chest and muscular shoulders. He sent me to wait in his office in the courthouse while he interviewed people in the bank. I flashed him a bright smile when he came into the office.

"Miss Terry, I know this has to be a difficult time for you. I'll try to keep my questions as short as possible."

Oops. I dropped the smile and put on a teary-but-trying-to-be-brave expression.

"The witnesses said that the robber just gave you a little nudge as he left the building, but you spun around and latched onto Pop Thomas like you were drowning. Can you explain that?"

I'd practiced the story in my head starting from the time when I entered the bank and ending when the sheriff came in. Beginning the story at the end left me a little off balance.

"I was terrified, Sheriff. I saw Pop and hung on for dear life."

"By grabbing Pop, you made sure he didn't follow the robber out of the bank. If it was on purpose, I'd like to thank you."

"You would?" I asked.

98

The Turkey Hill Affair

"Sure," he said. "Pop shouldn't be chasing bank robbers at his age. He'd only get himself shot. This way he's a hero and nobody got hurt."

Allen smiled. "He's been explaining to me why fighting in the trenches was tougher than landing on the beach on D-Day. From the way he's strutting around, I figure Mom Thomas might want to thank you tomorrow."

"I'm glad nobody got hurt," I said.

"The witnesses also told me that you and the bank robber chatted like old friends while he held you hostage. They said they couldn't hear well because you were talking so softly. What was it that you two talked about? Why did you talk so softly?"

I looked down at the floor before answering, "I was so scared that my mouth was dry. I don't know why the robber talked quietly. I begged him not to hurt me. He told me to do what he said."

Sheriff Allen nodded. "I wondered if it might be something like that, but the witnesses insisted that you two were gabbing away like you'd known each other for years. You know they're not big city people, but they're still pretty sharp."

Like you, I thought to myself.

He continued. "One odd thing is that you seemed to know what to do during a robbery better than he did. You bumped into him. He dropped his gun and the money. You picked up the gun first. You handed it to him instead of pointing it at him."

"He, uh, he was too close. He could have taken it from me. Somebody might have gotten shot in the process. Maybe me."

"I agree. That was good thinking. It's best to keep everybody safe. Next you picked up the money and handed that to him."

"He threatened me," I said.

"There's another odd thing," said the sheriff. "Nobody heard him say a word to you right then."

Then my mouth really got dry. I shrugged. "Maybe it was the expression on his face."

"The witnesses thought you started pushing him toward the door instead of the other way around."

I didn't like the implication of the questions.

"I swear to you on my life that I had no idea the bank was being robbed until I ran into that man. I had nothing to do with planning the robbery. I wasn't part of it. I did what I had to do and then I collapsed on the guard."

Sheriff Allen narrowed his eyes. He questioned me over and over again. At last he said, "It doesn't seem likely that you'd go waltzing into the bank to rob it dressed in high heels, a short skirt and a low-cut blouse. Even if you wore a mask, everybody would have known that you were the one who did it. No other woman in Lincoln County dresses like you do."

I smiled although I wasn't sure that was a compliment.

"I know Bob Tatum brought you back from New York to meet his parents. I took one look at you and I knew why. I've known Bob all his life. He's a fine man. I know he volunteered to be a medic the same day that I volunteered to fight the Nazis. What I don't know is why you would come here with him."

I thought for a moment. The sheriff was pretty sharp. I decided I'd be better off sticking to the facts. I sighed. "I have a loving nature. My boyfriend in New York, Frank, was not a nice man. To tell the truth, he ran a mob, and made money from politics, loan sharking and blackmail. Frank took advantage of my loving nature and snapped some photos of me loving some well-known people. He planned on hitting them up for dough, which, in the long run, didn't look good for me. Frank could take care of himself, but some heavy hitters might get it in their heads that they'd be safer if I was out of the picture, so to speak. So I hired a P.I. Somehow he got the negatives. I knew Frank would be upset. That could be really bad for my health. The P.I. worked faster than I expected. I needed to get away quickly and quietly. I knew I could trust Bob. He would never sell me out. So, I let him take me out of town."

"And Iowa isn't quite what you thought it would be."

It occurred to me that, as a combat veteran, the sheriff had seen plenty of things in Europe that his neighbors would never even dream about. He might have a more sophisticated attitude than most people in the area.

"Don't get me wrong. The Tatums are fine people and Bob is a real gentleman. I just don't know if I was cut out for living here. I've talked it over with Bob and he agrees that it would be best for both of us to just be friends. I expect to go back to New York pretty soon. As nice as this town is, the only ones here wearing tassels are the cornstalks."

"We don't have that many strippers," admitted Allen.

"I got excited when I heard about swap meets, but it's not where you meet and swap partners."

He added, "The only stud fees we pay around here are for pure-bred bulls."

I batted my eyes at him. "Once I really got my hopes up when Bob suggested that we sneak out to be together late at night. He said if I brought the bait, he'd bring the pole."

"Let me guess. He took you to his favorite fishing hole."

I nodded and stepped closer to him. "You know, Sheriff, I haven't lost that loving nature. I could show you sometime. You probably know where the haystacks are. We could go for a roll in the hay."

"I don't know if my wife would go along with that."

"Tell her she's invited, too."

Sheriff Allen smiled. "I might just do that. I wonder what she'd say."

"Take it from me, Sheriff, you'll never know until you ask."

"Miss Terry, I promise I will give that my full consideration. Let me get back to you on that."

I lowered my eyelids and looked at him through my lashes. I sighed. It was time to get back to business.

"Sheriff, can I ask you a question?"

"Sure thing."

"Do you think you can find the robber?"

"If he's anywhere in the area, I can."

"Why do you say that?"

"Miss Terry, there aren't many people in this part of the state. We take quite an interest in whoever is around, especially a stranger. I already put out bulletins. Unless the robber hightailed it out of here, sooner or later somebody will tell me where he is."

As planned, I met Bennie at ten on the deserted street outside the bank. I said, "The last time I saw you before the bank job, you were collecting debts for Frank. What are you doing here?"

"When you disappeared from New York, Frank got real mad. We looked all over for you. I came into his office early one morning and found the door to safe wide open. It was empty. Right then the cops busted down the door and told me Frank was dead. Some of the boys thought I had cleaned out the strong box."

The Turkey Hill Affair

"Maybe the cops took the blackmail photos."

"Nah, they would have sold them back to us. Cops don't have the patience to do decent blackmail work."

I had to admit that was true.

"It got so hot for me in New York that I had to hop a train. I came out to my granny's farm. I hide in the barn all day so nobody sees me. I can't go anywhere without stepping in pig shit. You're a smart girl, Roxie. Help me out. I thought if I robbed the bank, I might get enough money to get away or I might get sent to prison and meet somebody who can tell me what to do. I met Frank in prison and he let me work for him."

"How much money did you get?" I asked.

"Either almost eight hundred or almost nine hundred. I don't count so good. What should I do? I could leave here but, where would I go and what would I do when I got there?"

"First you need to give me the money."

Bennie hesitated. I raised my eyebrows.

"Do you want to figure this out on your own?" I asked.

Bennie handed over the sack. Why can't my boyfriends act like Bennie?

I said, "I'll talk to the sheriff. Maybe you can turn yourself in."

"I don't know," said Bennie. "I'm not a squealer, even on myself."

"Okay. Maybe he could catch you."

"That's better," he answered.

"Bennie, meet me here at the same time in two days. Let me see what I can arrange."

I stopped by the sheriff's office the next day.

"Did you make any progress on the robbery?" I asked.

"I'm starting to get reports about strangers. So far, they're

103

Murder Manhattan Style

just hoboes or folks passing through, but it won't take much longer. There is one more thing that's strange, though."

"What's that?"

"Carl Elkins, the bank president, estimated that the robber made off with twenty thousand dollars."

My legs felt shaky. I looked for a chair and sat down.

Sheriff Allen said, "You picked up that bag. Was it as big as the one Santa Claus carries?"

I shook my head.

The sheriff said, "I didn't think so. That much money wouldn't fit in a regular bag. I know that weeks ago the bank auditors scheduled a visit for next Friday. It seems to me that the bank is in trouble."

I asked, "Do you think that the bank president set up the robbery?"

"No. He's trying to take advantage of it. The bank records will sink him in the end. He's just stalling. My guess is that he's been making bad loans and taking a little out of the till for a long time. He's been on the phone all night, getting pledges from successful farmers and business owners. There's a reward of a thousand dollars for the capture of the robber."

"That's more than..." I started.

The sheriff raised his eyebrows. "More than?"

"More than enough to get people out carrying guns and looking for the robber. It could turn dangerous."

Sheriff Allen said, "I know, but what can I do about it?"

I thought about it. "I have an idea."

Thursday evening at five forty-two, Sarah Elkins left home to attend choir practice at Covenant Presbyterian Church. At five fifty, Bennie slipped through the back door of the banker's house with the sheriff and me close behind. Bennie walked quietly into

104

the library. Carl Elkins sat at his desk staring at a ledger.

Bennie said, "Which set of books is that, Mr. Banker?" He raised his gun. "Is that the one that shows how less than a thousand dollars becomes twenty thousand?"

Elkins pointed his finger at Bennie. "You're the robber."

"I'm one of the robbers," said Bennie. "I'm the one that used a gun. You're the one that cooked the books. As long as I'm on the hook for twenty thousand, I might as well have that much. Where is it?"

I was impressed that Bennie remembered what I told him to say.

"You fool," said Elkins. "It's long gone in bad loans and uncollectible bills."

Bennie laughed. "You're the fool if you think I believe that. The robbery gave you perfect cover to make another personal withdrawal. I'll take that money."

Elkins cursed.

Bennie said, "I could just kill you and search on my own."

Elkins said, "It's in the drawer to my right."

"Open the drawer slowly. Tell me now if there's a gun in there."

"Only money."

"Move away from the desk." Bennie walked to the desk and looked into the open drawer.

Elkins dived at Bennie, grabbed his wrist and wrenched the gun out of his hand. Panting heavily, Elkins turned the gun on Bennie.

"That's enough, Carl," said the sheriff, stepping into the room.

Elkins said, "It's the bank robber. I caught him sneaking into my house. He said he's already sent the money he took in the robbery to his friends out of state. He came here to kill me so I can't identify him."

"It won't work, Carl," said the sheriff. "I heard everything that the two of you said."

Elkins looked at the gun in his hand as if he had never seen it before. He lifted it slowly.

The sheriff said, "Carl, don't."

Elkins pointed the gun at Bennie. Then he swung it around toward Allen. With his hand shaking, he put the barrel in his mouth.

Sheriff Allen said, "Carl."

Elkins pulled the trigger. The hammer landed with a click on an empty chamber. Elkins dropped the gun and stood without moving while the sheriff handcuffed him.

When I came into the sheriff's office the next day, Bennie was in one of the cells, whistling while he tried to teach Elkins how to play slap jack. I dropped the sack of money from the bank on the sheriff's desk.

"How much is it?" asked the sheriff.

"Eight hundred thirty seven dollars," I said.

"A search of the house turned up less than that. I'll bet the audit will show that the bank didn't keep enough cash on hand. With the robbery solved, the FDIC will cover everybody's deposits. People will be okay. Thanks for talking Bennie into telling you where he hid the money. Thanks for bringing it in."

"I'll be satisfied with my half of the reward," I said.

Sheriff Allen smiled at me. "Half? I'm in law enforcement. I'm not eligible for the reward. You'll get the whole reward in the next couple of days. I expect you'll head back to New York after that."

"I suppose so," I said. "Bob is an awful nice guy, but I

don't think I'm a small town girl. With my old boyfriend out of the picture, there's nothing keeping me from going back to New York."

The sheriff said, "I'm glad you can stay or go as you please. Oh, my wife heard about the bank robbery. It must be the talk of the county. She asked me to invite you to dinner tonight."

I stepped closer to him and smiled. "And after dinner? For dessert?"

"As a beautiful, smart young woman from the big city once said to me, Roxie, you'll never know until you ask."

Author's note: Editor Ramona Long reviewed this story for inclusion in an anthology by the Sisters in Crime subgroup known as Guppies. The anthology has not yet been published. She helped make this a much better story. Thank you, Ramona.

Author's note: One of the highlights of every conclave has been the law enforcement panel, when people involved in all aspects of enforcement discuss issues between themselves and willingly answer any question thrown at them from the audience. It's rare to have the opportunity to listen to such a wide range of experts. Although the membership of the panel has varied a bit over the years, it has included Director of the Riley County Police Department Mike Watson, RCPD investigator Alan "Rhino" Riniker, 30-year FBI veteran and mystery writer of note Mark Bouton, and forensic anthropologist Dr. Michael Finnegan. Other panelists have included prosecuting and defense attorneys and a forensic psychologist. The panelists are knowledgeable, friendly, and, as you can see from the short story that follows, good sports.

Murder at the GMMC

Manhattan, Kansas, Present Day

When the phone rang at two in the morning, it wrenched me out of a dreamless sleep. I peered into the unfamiliar gloom trying to remember where I was. Manhattan. Kansas, of course. I was at the second Great Manhattan Mystery Conclave where, wonder of wonders, my short story had been included in the *Manhattan Mysteries* anthology launched the day before. Until then, I had one novel published after a mere nine years of trying, which qualified me as an overnight success, garnered stellar reviews and produced sales in the high tens. (Thank God for independent bookstores like Claflin Books and Copies and I Love a Mystery and kind people like Stormy Kennedy and Becci West, who know their readers well enough to recommend an unknown author like me, or I would have no sales outside my family.) Sales in the tens of original books, that is. Used book sales benefit neither me nor my publisher. The used book market took off just when the spread of SARS reached epidemic proportions. Coincidence? I don't think so.

What was that annoying noise? The phone. I reached for the phone, backhanding the clock radio half off the nightstand and stinging my knuckles. I managed to say, "Uh."

An obviously disguised voice announced, "I'm going to kill you. Sorry to wake you up. Sweet dreams." There was a click followed by a dial tone.

"'S all right," I answered. "I was awake anyway 'cause the phone rang."

At seven in the morning, the phone rang with my wake-up call. I thanked the recorded voice before recalling the strange dream from last night. Then I noticed that the clock radio was half off the nightstand.

Who would want to kill me and why? I'm middle aged (assuming I live to be one hundred twelve), balding, monogamous and solvent. In other words – boring. I'm a psychologist in my day job. The only thing unusual about me is that I write well and I have the delusion that someone will pay to publish my writing. Could that be it? I resolved to ask other authors with stories in *Manhattan Mysteries* if they got similar threats.

At breakfast I sat at a table with some of my fellow authors, although not many of the authors were fellows.

"I see you remembered to wear your rosette award," said Beth Groundwater, touching the ribbon of hers.

"Yes, I figured out I was supposed to wear it during the conclave just as soon as you told me."

"I hope we weren't too hard on you last night," said Linda Berry. "We have to take into account your inherited gender disadvantage."

"Testosterone poisoning. At least I chose an orange rosette so it will go with anything I wear. I've been telling people I won it at the county fair for best sweet pickles. Listen, I got a phone call early this morning threatening to kill me. I was wondering if you got similar calls."

They exchanged knowing looks.

"We were just discussing that," said Beth. "We did but we decided not to say anything unless you asked. It could be a prank. We asked Margaret Shauers and she said she got a threatening call."

"If anyone is killed, she should go first," said Linda.

"I agree. She had three stories accepted. If they didn't have the rule limiting the number of submissions you could make, it would have been the Margaret Shauers anthology."

Beth said, "Jerry A. Peterson should go next. He had two accepted. Marolyn Caldwell and Robin Higham collaborated on two. Does that put them third and fourth, or does it just count as one each?"

Linda said, "I vote for them getting knocked off third and fourth."

"Sounds fair to me."

Beth said, "Maybe the killer will start alphabetically."

Linda said, "Then I'd go first. I prefer to think the assassin will use the order the stories are in." She smiled at me. My story was first. Hers was last.

"I think we should at least mention it to Marolyn. She's an author as well as the organizer of all this."

After breakfast I headed out to my car to put copies of the anthology into my trunk. I noticed a man nearby who had the hood up on a white Honda Accord. It looked just like mine. He was even in a parking space I used for most of yesterday before a space opened closer to my room. He slammed the hood but I didn't hear it close. That was because of the explosion and the fireball that engulfed the man and the car. I was knocked off my feet and I nearly dropped the books. As I lost consciousness, I muttered to myself, "I'm definitely talking to Marolyn."

I awoke in a hospital bed some time later. Eventually the ringing in my ears quieted down enough for me to talk to the police. I recognized Alan Riniker of the Riley County Police Department and the department director, Mike Watson, from a law enforcement seminar at the conclave. I described what I had seen.

Alan said, "Who would want to kill you?"

"Nobody I know of but I did get a threatening phone call around two in the morning."

Alan said, "Did it occur to you to call the police?"

"I just told you."

Mike cleared his throat. "The deceased has been identified as a local gentleman with ties to the Kansas Konspiracy, spelled with a K."

"Who are they?"

Mike said, "They left the Klu Klux Klan when they thought it became too liberal. They commit crimes to make money. The deceased apparently was trying to rig a pipe bomb to explode when the motor started."

Alan snorted. "He was dumber than a box of rocks. The car he blew up belonged to an eighty-five-year-old Sunday school teacher. We think he was after you. Do you know anyone in the mob?"

"No. And I don't know anyone who'd want to kill me or any reason someone would want me dead."

Mike said, "We checked with all the contest winners who got stories into the anthology. They all got threatening calls. Apparently no one else did. We think that's a cover for someone who wants to kill one of the winners. Maybe you. We're checking on the writers who got turned down to cover all the bases. It doesn't make sense to us that someone whose story was not accepted would be so upset that he or she would try to kill the winners."

"You're not writers, are you?"

They questioned me about my time in Manhattan. I missed the tour of the town early in the morning and arrived in time to attend the seminar by the Deadly Divas. Sadly, this year they didn't wear tiaras and boas. Denise Swanson talked about creating a character. Marcia Talley offered information on references and writing. Letha Albright told us about chasing dreams. The founder of the group, Susan McBride, defined Chick Lit and gave fashion tips. I asked her why she was known as the "Chanteuse of Chick Lit."

She answered, "I think they mean chartreuse. It is one of my colors."

"I talked to her alone later about making book signings into events. She had some great ideas."

"You can skip telling us that part," said Alan, rolling his eyes.

"I spent the rest of the afternoon at the Prairie Tea to launch *Manhattan Mysteries.* I met Nancy Pickard and Marcia Talley, two of the judges. I saw the bookstore owner who sponsored my first book signing, chatted with the other authors, ate entirely too much and rode back to the motel in the van."

Alan asked, "So at the tea and afterward, you were never alone? The killer didn't have a clean shot at you?"

"I guess not."

Alan asked, "What did you do that evening?"

"I talked with writers sitting around the lobby. That was the best part of the conclave. I suggested book titles to Carolyn Hart and Shirley Damsgaard. The rest of the evening I talked to Linda Berry and Beth Groundwater. Other people stopped by from time to time. Margaret Shauers, Pamela Fesler and Michelle Mach joined us at different times. I don't know if any of this is helpful."

Mike said, "Neither do we. Unlike in mystery books, real police work consists of gathering lots of mostly useless information and doing paperwork. We keep asking questions and eventually, piece by piece, we find out what we need to know."

"There's a meeting tonight with the judges to talk about publicity. The doctor says I can go. If you're done with your questioning, I'd like to get dressed and get back so I can attend it. I hope you're covering the meeting. All the threatened people will be together in one place."

Alan shook his head. "I still think the threats are a distraction. Someone is out to kill one of the winning authors. The car bomb might be a distraction, too. We're spending time with you instead of investigating the rest of the writers. Maybe one of the writers wants to kill another one. As far as we can tell, nobody wants to kill you."

"That's good to hear."

I got back to the motel where the charred husk of the bombed-out car still sat behind crime scene tape. I shivered when I thought it could have been my car with me in it. Alan's words were not as reassuring when confronted with the wreckage.

To my surprise, Susan McBride met me just outside the door.

"Hi, there," she said.

I jumped. "Sorry, I didn't see you in that black outfit. You were in something bright red and shimmering during your seminar."

Before she could answer, a group of Kansas State football fans burst out of the door singing and laughing. They flipped a football toward Susan and cheered when she caught it. She tossed it to me and I passed it back to them. They marched away singing their fight song.

Susan said, "How nice of you to notice. I heard you were in the hospital. I hope you're all right. What happened?"

"I'm just bruised and battered, thanks. Somebody blew himself up and I was too close. Apparently he was putting a pipe bomb in a car. I think it was a failed hit."

She nodded, "There are easier ways to commit suicide. Whoever hired him must be upset. It just goes to show how hard it is to get good help these days."

"Especially out of town where you don't know anyone."

"Too true. You have to do everything yourself. I'm glad you're not hurt." She slipped away silently.

The painkillers they gave me in the hospital were wearing off as I limped down the hall toward Conference Room IV. When I entered the room, the judges – Carolyn Hart, Nancy

Murder Manhattan Style

Pickard and Marcia Talley – started to applaud. My fellow authors joined in. I noticed that Margaret Shauers was especially pleased. Then I remembered that one of her stories was second in the anthology. If the killer was using the order of the stories in the book, she was safe as long as I survived. The applause stopped. Everyone stared past me. I turned around to see Susan McBride, carrying a black pistol with a long barrel. I stared at the gun.

She said, "Don't you think it matches my outfit?"

I nodded without speaking.

She said, "I do want to apologize to you. I meant to kill you, but I didn't mean for you to suffer. And I have good news."

She smiled brightly.

"I was going to kill the contest winners one at a time. There is too just much competition writing mysteries and too few publishers. But I've changed my mind."

We applauded. She gave a neat curtsy.

She continued. "Why should I worry about people who are mostly just starting out when I can kill three authors who are at the top? The best publishers will be begging for experienced authors."

She turned the gun toward the judges. "Carolyn Hart, they call you America's Agatha Christie. You were nominated for a Pulitzer Prize. That never happens for a mystery. Nancy Pickard, you won an American Mystery Award, an Agatha, an Anthony, a Macavity and a Shamus. Is there anything you haven't won?"

Nancy answered, "An Edgar."

Susan shook her head, "You've been nominated three times. You'll win it for sure, if you survive."

She turned the gun toward Marcia Talley. "You are the new hot author. You won an Agatha and an Anthony. Malice

116

Domestic gave you a writing grant. Getting paid before you finish a book? I can't forgive that."

Wincing in pain, I limped toward her. "Susan, you can't be serious. Tell us it's a joke. We'll all laugh and forget the whole thing."

She swung around to face me, turning her back to the judges. "Don't push it. You're lucky to be alive."

"You don't want to kill me." I limped closer. "You already had at least two chances and you let me live."

She said, "Don't come any closer."

"I talked to you alone after your seminar. You could have killed me then and no one would have known."

She snapped, "Idiot. Think back to what I was wearing. Something bright red and shimmering, remember? It was fine silk and not colorfast. It is impossible to get bloodstains out of that material. Men!"

"Outside the motel?"

"Remember the football fans? They noticed me. I mean, who wouldn't? But still they got a good look at me with you. Why take the chance?"

I exhaled. "This outfit?"

She said, "It's an easy-care fabric. Besides, I'm tired of it already."

"If you kill the judges, the authors will be witnesses."

Susan said, "So I lied about not killing all of you. So you've gone from the prime target to collateral damage. So arrest me."

"Freeze!" Susan turned her head toward where the judges had been. Two police officers in uniform and Alan stood pointing their weapons at Susan.

"Drop the gun!"

With a graceful move, she bent her knees, laid the gun on the floor and then rose again. An officer handcuffed her and started to read from a small card. "You are under arrest...."

You could have warned me," I said to Alan. "When I saw the officers emerge from hiding, I nearly jumped out of my skin."

He said, "We didn't know for sure if you were part of her plan. You wouldn't have behaved normally if you'd been clued in."

"So you used me as bait without my knowledge."

He said, "Yep. Got a problem with that?"

"It works for me. You know, I've never written about true crime. As witness to the events with no need for an 'as told to,' this has definite possibilities."

Authors note: People named in the story have given their consent to be mentioned. Keep in mind this is just a story. My life is not as interesting as depicted here, but then again, it's not as dangerous and painful, either.

Locard's Principle

Manhattan, Kansas, Present Day

It didn't matter that she was dead. Every time the phone rang, I expected to hear Margaret's voice. When I heard footsteps behind me, I turned around, expecting to see her. I found myself staring at women who resembled Margaret only slightly.

Whoever it was that broke into our home, robbed us and smashed her head open also killed half of me. That half that sang along with the radio, laughed and loved was gone. I didn't think he would ever return. I ate. I went to work in the lab, although at the end of the day I had no idea what I had done. I tried to sleep and sometimes succeeded. I listened dully while some friends fumbled around trying to express their sympathy. Other so-called friends turned and almost ran when they saw me coming, like I was carrying the plague.

I was sitting at home watching "Dora the Explorer" when the phone rang. I was watching a kid's show because all the other channels showed couples or police officers or something else I could not watch without crying. I stared at the phone. There wasn't any reason to answer it; the only person I wanted to talk to would never call me again. The phone kept ringing. The noise bothered me. I answered it.

"Dr. Willis, this is Detective Norris."

Murder Manhattan Style

I remembered that when he questioned me about Margaret's murder, he'd been sympathetic and sincere.

"I wanted you to know, sir, that we arrested a man we believe killed your wife."

I wondered why that mattered, but I spoke to him because that's what people do when they answer the phone.

"Thanks for letting me know. Why do you think that he's the one who killed Margaret?"

"The suspect is no rocket scientist. We think he was looking for things he could steal to support his drug habit. He apparently panicked when your wife heard him and came downstairs. We believe he picked up a glass vase and hit her. We found the vase with his fingerprints and her blood on it. The fingerprints gave us his identity. Searching his apartment under a warrant, we found her blood on his shoes, a shirt and a pair of pants that he wore. Apparently he tried to wash it off, but he did a lousy job. When we brought him in, he as much as admitted that he killed her before he remembered to lawyer up. The courts will decide if he's guilty or not, of course, but I wanted you to know he's in custody."

"Thank you, Detective." I hung up. My pulse started to pound. I began to sweat. I felt something again – rage.

The next step seemed obvious. After all, I was already half dead. There was one thing to accomplish before I made myself completely dead. Because of the pain he caused me I was entitled, almost obligated, to kill the murderer. I switched to a local channel. I didn't have to wait long. Action News gave a breathless report of the arrest. They had his name and photos of his face. They said the preliminary hearing of the alleged killer was scheduled for the day after tomorrow at the courthouse.

At the university lab the next day I considered the problem.

Locard's Principle

The courthouse must have metal detectors. But then again, what did I know about guns or knives? I didn't want to hurt some innocent bystander. It didn't take long to find a non-metallic, quick-acting lethal solution. I made just enough of what I needed for him and for me. I envisioned how close I needed to get and practiced the actions I would take. I knew that I could not be absolutely certain he would die, but the probability was high. If he lived, he would be in great pain. No one could stop me from killing myself. If the paramedics wasted time trying to revive me, that would delay treatment of the suspect.

When I said I wouldn't be in the next day, nobody asked any questions. I carried what I needed out of the lab in my lunch sack inside two thick polystyrene vials. The lids would flip open with a tap of the thumb.

I slept better that night than I had since Margaret died. The next morning I dressed in a suit, opened my briefcase and placed several professional articles I had never gotten around to reading over the two vials. As I expected, at the courthouse I passed through the metal detectors without a problem. They didn't even make me open the briefcase. I snagged one of the chairs in the hall, opened the briefcase and slipped the vials into a coat pocket. I kept my head down as if I were reading articles, glancing up occasionally to see if the suspect was coming.

An influx of camera crews and grim police officers let me know that he would be along soon. I snapped the briefcase closed and joined the people watching the news crews. I fingered the vials in my pocket and mentally rehearsed the actions I had planned. Pull out one vial. Pop off the lid. Step toward him. When as close as possible, throw the contents in his face. Drop the first vial. Pull out the second. Open it. Swallow the contents.

Murder Manhattan Style

"Dr. Willis."

Startled, I turned toward the voice. I saw a stoop-shouldered man in a rumpled suit. He had sad brown eyes.

"Hello, Detective Norris," I said.

"We brought the suspect in earlier through a side entrance. He's in a heavily guarded courtroom. Nobody but court officials or the police can get close to him. Why don't you come with me?"

I took my hand out of my jacket pocket, picked up my briefcase and followed him down the hall. He led me into a small cluttered office.

The detective said, "I'm not going to ask you why you're here. I wouldn't want you to have to lie to me. I'm not even going to ask you what you have in your coat pocket."

"How did you know about that?"

"When I see a bereaved husband waiting where the man accused of killing his wife is supposed to be and fiddling with something in his pocket, I become very curious. I'm not going to be too nosy this time, but there better not be a second time."

I shook my head. A tightness I had not been aware of eased in my chest. "There won't be. I'll never be able to get up the nerve to try again."

Norris said, "Good. I believe you. Still, I want you to stay away from the courthouse until this is all over."

I nodded and stood up to leave.

"There is one thing," said Norris. "Did you ever hear of Edmond Locard?"

"No. Is he associated with this case?"

Norris smiled. "I suppose he is, in a general way. Edmond Locard was a scientist, like you. Maybe that's why I thought about him. At the beginning of the twentieth century, he figured out how many points of agreement were needed to be certain that two fingerprints came from the same person. He pioneered the use of trace evidence. He's most famous for what we call Locard's Principle."

"What's that?"

"Locard said that wherever someone goes, whatever someone touches, he leaves behind some trace of himself and he picks up some trace of where he's been and what he's touched."

I said, "Like the suspect who left fingerprints behind and picked up drops of Margaret's blood on his clothing."

Norris said, "Exactly. Well, over the years I've come to believe that the principle applies to more than physical evidence. It applies to emotion and, I don't know, something in the universe in general. I can't explain it well. I'm just a cop. I do know that the suspect didn't just kill your wife. He kicked a big hole in your life too and hurt a lot of people that she touched.

"I believe that if you did something back to him, you'd be causing pain to everyone that he touched. He might be a miserable excuse for a human being but he has a family and friends who knew him before he became a junkie. I can't even imagine how you feel, but I don't think you'd want to make anyone else feel that way."

I shook my head.

Norris said, "Killing yourself would hurt those who were closest to your wife. You still touch a lot of people who Margaret touched. Would you want their memories of her haunted by your actions? Can't you hear them say, 'Do you know what Margaret's husband did?' I can."

He left quietly while I wept.

I didn't follow the trial of the accused. I declined to talk to reporters about it. After all, it had nothing to do with me.

Murder Manhattan Style

Sometimes now, well-meaning friends ask me if I've come to terms with Margaret's murder. I don't know what that means. I don't expect to. Recently I've started to meet once in a while with Margaret's parents at their house. Sometimes her brother and her sisters drop by. We talk about how she touched us all. We touch each other.

Author's note: I got the idea for this story from a presentation by the director of the Kansas City Police Department crime lab at the Kansas City Sisters in Crime chapter named Partners in Crime.

Riding Shotgun

Manhattan, Kansas, Present Day

I was in disguise when it started – designer sunglasses, boat shoes without socks and a tailored Italian suit. I was wandering around a high-class restaurant district called Plaza West, waiting for someone to act like an idiot. That's how I made a living.

I figured out a long time ago that I'm not the sharpest pencil in the box. I will never have a job where I wear a suit and tie and talk to people in my air-conditioned office. The jobs I can get leave grease under my fingernails and calluses on my hands. I thought it would always be like that, but one night when I was in jail after sleeping off a drinking binge, I met a man who told me a way to make a living that didn't involve heavy lifting.

I was looking for the chance to work when, just outside a restaurant named Mosaics, a trophy wife with a figure like an ad for plastic surgery and a face like a Noxzema commercial acted like an idiot right in front of me. She didn't bother to park her car and lock it before walking into the restaurant. She hopped out of her new black Toyota 4Runner and jogged in, leaving the keys in the ignition with the motor running. As if this had been worked out ahead of time, I waved at her retreating back, opened the door and slid in. I took a moment to adjust the mirrors (in my line of work it's good to know who's behind you). Then I signaled before pulling away from the curb and merged into traffic.

Some days I love my job. Driving like a little old lady on Sunday, I could be at the chop shop within fifteen minutes where, on an average day, a car is searched for tracking devices, stripped of identification, and broken down into parts before the owner calms down enough to tell the police what they need to know. Because tire tread can be used for identification, tires are out of the shop within minutes.

At a red light, I pulled out my cell phone to call ahead and alert the crew.

"Hi!" came from the back seat. With a sinking heart, I turned my head to see a girl with curly blond hair and bright blue eyes sitting in the middle of the back seat. She looked like a ten-year-old version of the trophy wife.

"Where in blazes did you come from?" I asked.

"I knew you'd be shocked," she said. "I waited for a red light so you wouldn't crash the car. I was on the floor in the back seat reading my book when my mom went into the restaurant. She was stupid to leave the keys in the car."

Someone honked. I looked at the light. It had turned green so I drove forward.

"Don't worry," I said. "I won't hurt you. I wouldn't have taken the car if I'd seen you. Let's see, Manhattan Christian College is not far away. I can drop you off outside the main office. If you go in and tell them what happened, they'll let you use the phone to call your mom."

"No way. I'll scream."

"There's no reason to be afraid," I said. "I promise I won't hurt you. I'll pull over and let you out right here if you want."

"No!"

I said. "Okay, you win. You keep the car. I'll pull into a

parking lot, give you the keys and walk away."

I'd have to wipe my fingerprints off the steering wheel and the keys. There might be hair and fibers for the cops to find, but I could trash the suit and move out of town if I had to. I wondered if evidence labs could really do the things you see on television. My crime was only grand theft auto. Maybe they wouldn't bother.

"Noooo! You don't get it. You're not paying attention. I don't want the car. I don't want you to drop me off."

"What do you want?" I asked.

"I don't want to go home. I want to stay with you." She burst into tears. Her body shook.

"This could only happen to me," I muttered under my breath. "Stop crying. You can't stay with me. For all you know, I might be an ax murderer or something."

"You promised you wouldn't hurt me. I believe you. Being with you has to be better than living where I am."

"Little girl...."

"Susie."

"Susie," I said, "listen to me. When your mother reports you missing, there's going to be a firestorm. A description of this car and its license plate number will be all over television and radio. Your picture will be, too. We don't have much time."

Susie said, "Pull into that parking garage."

"Okay, but we can't hide there for very long." I did as she asked.

"We're not hiding," said Suzie. "There's a screwdriver in the back. You can switch plates with another car. Look, some cars are parked in reserved spaces. The drivers probably won't come out until work is over. If it's dark when they come out, they may not notice the switch until morning. Don't worry. There are tons of cars just like this one."

I would never have thought of it, but it made sense to me. I did what Susie advised while she acted as lookout. We had new plates in no time.

"Come on," I said. "Tell me what this is about. You can ride shotgun."

"What does that mean?" she asked.

"You can ride in the front seat next to me. In the old days when they had stagecoaches, a guard with a shotgun would ride next to the driver. In my family, the first kid to claim shotgun got to ride in the front seat. You're my guard. I'm counting on you to protect me. Watch out for police cars. Check behind us from time to time and let me know if we're being followed."

"I'll put on sunglasses," said Susie. "Maybe I could wear a disguise."

"Yeah, we'll get you a long white beard."

Susie giggled. She jumped into the car and bounced up and down on the seat. I looked at her before starting the engine.

"Put on your seatbelt."

"You see," she crowed, "you don't want me to get hurt. You're not an ax murderer."

"Lucky for you," I answered. "Now tell me what this is about. What's so terrible at home that you think you'd be better off with a criminal?"

"What can I call you? I have to call you something."

"How about Jesse?"

"Like Jesse James? Cool," she said. "I could be Belle Starr."

"Well, Susie or Belle, tell me what's so bad at home."

She hesitated. "If I tell you, will you make it better?"

"I don't know if I can," I answered. "Maybe I could help

some. I don't know 'cause I don't know what you're talking about."

She smiled. "Now I know you're honest, too. I already tried telling some people, but they couldn't help."

"Yep, I'm an honest car thief and I'll end up in prison someday. So quit stalling and tell me."

Susie scrunched up her forehead. In a small voice she asked, "Do you think I'm pretty?"

"Um, sure," I said. "You look like your mom. She's very pretty."

"My mom went to the doctor to get bigger boobies," said Susie.

"I bet she was pretty before that," I answered.

Susie leaned toward me and stared at me. "If you could date me or my mom, who would you date?"

"Date? I'm confused. You mean like hugging and kissing?"

"And other stuff, too," said Susie.

"No offense, Susie," I said, "but what kind of question is that? Grown-up men date grown-up women, not little girls. If I was your age, I'd be real happy to be your boyfriend, but we wouldn't go on dates. We might hold hands."

"You'd better pull over here," said Susie.

I stopped the car. "You better just tell me," I said. "I know you can tell that I'm not exactly an Einstein. Just say it."

Susie took a deep breath and then talked so quickly that the words ran together, "My step-dad tries to peek when I don't have any clothes on. He talks to me and says he's gonna do stuff to me like they do on dates. Twice he tried to touch me in places.... you know."

I did know and it made me feel sick.

"What does your mom say?"

"She says he's just joking, but he isn't."

"Did you tell a teacher?"

"I tried, but she didn't want to listen. My step-dad's rich and I go to a school where he pays them a lot of money. I don't know if the principal would believe me. Besides, it's embarrassing."

"Your step-dad's the one who should be embarrassed, not you. You didn't do anything wrong," I said. "What about your real dad?"

"I don't know where he is. I bet he really hates me because he never comes to see me, so he can't help."

"It might not be like that," I said. "I know this guy. He's a friend of mine. When he was young and dumb, he got a girl pregnant. Her family didn't like him. You can't blame them for that. He was kind of wild and he wasn't ready to be a father. He tried to settle down, but they didn't want him around the baby. The mom had a chance to go to school and become a doctor, but that meant she and the baby would move away. He could have gotten a lawyer and fought to make them stay. He could have moved to the place she was going, but that would have made it harder for the mom. In the end, he let them go without him. What would the baby have thought about having a dad who worked in a tire factory, got drunk on weekends and went to jail? It was hard, but he thought it was the best thing. He talked to the girl's dad, who was a cop, and they agreed he would leave them alone. The cop was pretty decent about it, really. He didn't threaten or yell. He just listened and talked."

"Does your friend miss them?"

"Oh, yes. All the time."

"The baby might not mind when she got older."

Riding Shotgun

"He, not she," I said. "It's way too late now. He's ten and a half and he's never known his dad. The mom married a nice guy. They're better off without him." I cleared my throat and blew my nose. Then I thought for a long time. "I wish we were Jesse and Belle. We'd just shoot the varmint." I reached for my wallet and pulled out a battered business card. "Back when, um, back when I started this racket, Detective Phillips came to see me. He said he knew I was the one stealing cars. He told me they'd catch me sooner or later. I knew he was right. He told me if I ever got in a real fix, I should give him a call."

I dialed the number and eventually got connected to Phillips.

"Are you looking for a little girl named Susie and a black Toyota 4Runner? I can get them to you, but you have to promise to listen to the girl before anything else. You have to listen to her before you let her parents know she's there."

"The little girl is my top priority," said Phillips.

"I'm on the way there."

Susie looked sad and worried.

"Detective Phillips is a good man. He'll do anything he can to help you."

"What about you?"

"I'll be fine. I guess my car rustling days are over. Grand theft auto is a class C felony so it's not a walk in the park, but just about everybody I know has been in prison at one time or another. I'll survive. I'll spend a few years making license plates. With time off for good behavior, I'll be back out pretty soon. Besides, I'm going to return the car as good as new. That might count for something when I come up for parole."

When we pulled up at the police station, Susie was reluctant to get out of the car.

131

Murder Manhattan Style

"See," I said, "no parents. Phillips is a straight shooter." We went inside. Phillips was waiting. Susie asked me to stay with her so I did. He listened to Susie's story about her stepfather without interrupting her and then called somebody he knew at Family Services.

"We will investigate this before we decide when it's safe for you to go home. I promise you that," Phillips said and leaned back in the chair. "Now tell me about the carjacking."

"Oh," said Susie. "It was very exciting. This very tall man with a white beard – I think it was a disguise – jumped in the car and drove off when Mom left it running at the restaurant."

My jaw dropped.

Susie continued, "He didn't know I was there. I was scared so I hid. He stopped in a parking garage of an office building, got out and did something to the front and back of the car. He took off again. I was afraid he'd drive far away so finally I let him know I was there. When I popped up, he pulled the car into a parking lot and ran off without the keys."

She smiled at me. "This nice man here asked if I was in trouble and I told him everything. He called you and drove us here."

Phillips looked at me. "If you don't close your mouth, you'll catch a fly in there." He looked back at Susie. "You know we can dust the car for fingerprints."

"He was wearing leather gloves."

"The tall man was?"

"Very tall with a white beard. I think it was a disguise."

Phillips looked at me.

"Did you see that very tall man?"

Susie nudged me with her foot.

"No. The only person I saw in the car was Susie."

Riding Shotgun

"Why am I not surprised by that?" asked Phillips. "You and I are going to have a very long talk. You are about to change careers. Have no doubt about that."

He turned toward Susie. "First, though, Susie, I need to take you to a children's shelter. If you like, we can go in a squad car."

"Cool," said Susie. "I'll ride shotgun."

Author's note: My own personal Java Judy likes this story very much. She suggested that I include it in this collection. People either really like or really dislike the hero. I expect that someday he'll tell me another story.

Hamlet, P.I.: Prince, Investigator of Denmark

Manhattan, Kansas, Present Day

Maybe I should have just bitten my tongue. But I looked at the oddly dressed customer in front of me, thought about the motto of MacGuffin Books and Sundries – *Sell Something!* – and plunged ahead. I said, "I've described our entire list of mystery bestsellers to you. If you don't want to read about a holistic healer who detects through reading crystals, a psychic parrot who's the reincarnation of the Black Dahlia, a geriatric ninja, or a snide schnauzer, what sort of mysteries do you like?"

The customer, a small pale man dressed in a long black coat with an enormous bow tie over a ruffled shirt, spoke in a soft Southern accent: "I want to read about a man who tries to stay true to himself in a corrupt world but never gets an even break. He's in despair as those in power plot against him, but he persists, knowing he will probably lose or even die at the end."

I looked at his burning dark eyes and said, "That sounds like something in the noir genre, or *Hamlet*, for that matter."

The man replied, "I think I've heard of that somewhere. Is there a dame in it?"

"Yes, but the relationship ends badly."

"Does the hero crack wise?"

"Some of his lines are downright famous."

135

"Tell me about it."

"You should know that it's a play, not a novel," I said. "It was written so long ago that the language can be quite hard to understand."

"And it's still in print?"

"It's considered a classic," I assured him. "It starts with Hamlet, Prince of Denmark, suspecting that his father has been murdered. He comes to the royal court to investigate. The murderer plots against him and Hamlet's not sure who he can trust. At the end, the stage is knee-deep in bodies."

He said, "I'll take it."

When he returned an hour later, I steeled myself to explain our no-return policy, but he didn't want his money back. He wanted to talk about the play.

He said, "You were right about the language, but, you know, it's almost poetic."

"I think so, too."

"So who do you think the ghost is?"

I answered, "Pardon?"

"You don't believe in ghosts, do you?"

"Well, no."

"Me, neither. So somebody has to be pretending to be the ghost."

I thought for a moment. "I've never considered that. But it would have to be somebody who looks like the dead king."

He nodded. "Exactly. But not the dead king himself. I don't see how he could have faked his own death. I like this. It's subtle."

He settled into one of our upholstered chairs and opened the book. He came back to the desk when I was ringing up a sale of an annotated edition of Sherlock Holmes with emphases on entomology and etymology.

Hamlet, P.I.: Prince, Investigator of Denmark

He said, "I'm sure the wandering players are a clue. I can't see it working out between Ophelia and Hamlet. Something bad is bound to happen there. Do you think Gertrude was in on the hit?"

"As I recall, at that point in the play it's hard to know. A doll in heat isn't the most logical person on earth, if you know what I mean. Not that a guy in heat is any better. You can see why Claudius was tempted."

He said, "I liked the part where Hamlet thought Claudius was praying and spared his life, but Claudius could not repent and could not pray."

"I've always thought that scene gives Claudius a conscience and makes him a much more interesting killer. It seems to me that, if Hamlet had killed him, in the eyes of the people Claudius would have become the martyred king and Hamlet would have become the mad assassin. I think Hamlet wants the world to know what Claudius did."

The man retreated to the chair but popped up again almost immediately. "Hamlet's in the soup now. He stabbed through the curtain not knowing who was behind it and killed an innocent man. You can understand it with all the pressure he's been under, but you can't forgive it."

"And Hamlet can't forgive himself."

He left the counter just long enough for me to set up a book signing with an author known for writing mysteries that Houdini solved by consulting the spirit world. When the customer returned, he was breathing hard.

"Betrayal, madness, drowning and pirates," he panted. "This scribbler, Shakespeare, doesn't miss a trick. Hamlet must know that the so-called 'playing' with foils with the son of the man he murdered is a trap."

137

"But he's going to do it anyway."

"I've almost got the identity of the ghost worked out. At first I thought it was Horatio."

I pondered for a moment and shook my head. "He was the least likely candidate, but I can't say I ever really doubted his loyalty."

He said, "I thought he might have been boffing Gertrude, too, but that didn't work as a motive. It was just a passing thought. Then I thought it might have been the school chums, but they were red herrings. Now, I have my sights on somebody else. I'll let you know if I was right."

"I can hardly wait." I honestly couldn't. I sold three books in the series about the Apostle Paul being a Roman spy before the customer appeared once more.

"Who do you think is the ghost?" he demanded.

"I really don't have a clue."

"I admit there aren't a lot of clues. However, I think Shakespeare was fair to his readers. Who's the most dangerous man in the play?"

"Claudius?"

"No, the only man he killed was asleep."

I thought about it. "Hamlet?"

"You're getting closer. I wouldn't want to cross swords with that mug. What do those two have in common?"

"Family, royalty, a claim to the throne."

"Precisely. One other person has all of those." He winked at me. "That character ends up with everything."

"The guy from Norway. Fortinbras? No way. He was such a minor character. He was hardly ever on stage."

"Think back. In the beginning of the play we learn that Hamlet's father, also named Hamlet, defeated Fortinbras's father, also named Fortinbras, in single combat and won lands away from Norway. We learn that Fortinbras is raising an army and might be trying to get his lands back. Well, he is. All the royal families were related. With makeup, Fortinbras looks like the dead king. He sends Hamlet off on a course that will end in disaster. If he can pretend to be the dead king, he can pretend to be one of the players, too. He enacts the murder with such detail that Claudius cannot stand to see it. That solidifies Hamlet's resolve to kill Claudius. Where does the poisoned foil come from? Fortinbras again. He has arms to supply his army. Then he shows up at the end and waltzes away with the Danish throne.

"I think his plan was that either Claudius would kill Hamlet or Hamlet would kill Claudius. Either way, Denmark would be weakened and her people would be left divided and dispirited. The country would be ripe for the picking. Hamlet and Claudius killed each other. Fortinbras won without a single battle."

I shook my head. "As many times as I've read *Hamlet,* that never occurred to me."

He smiled again. "I like this Shakespeare guy. Do you have anything else by him?"

"There is one play that actors consider cursed. They don't refer to it by name; they call it 'The Scottish Play'."

His eyes lit up. "Cursed?"

"It has everything Hamlet has, plus witches."

He said, "I want it."

I sold him an embossed leather-bound limited edition of *Macbeth,* leaned over the counter and whispered, "In the third scene of the third act, watch for the third murderer."

Author's note: *I want to acknowledge my debt to James Thurber and his short story "Macbeth Murder Mystery." I first*

Murder Manhattan Style

read the story in junior high school and thought at the time I could steal his plot. It took me several years, but I did and I think it turned out quite well in the end. I love the tag line for this story in Futures Mystery Anthology Magazine – *The Bard tells the dark tale of a Dane and a dame.*

Author's note: The next two stories have different settings and unique protagonists.

Heidegger's Cat

What do you say to a man whose son just died? How do you explain that, even if his son was your college roommate, you hardly knew him? Some university housing flunky had thought it would be a good joke to have Charles, who'd traveled extensively in Africa and Europe, room with me, a kid who had rarely been out of the ghetto. When Mr. Adeleye called and said he wanted to meet with Charles's friend, Tweener, and me, I couldn't think of a way to refuse. I told him I didn't know how to contact Tweener, but he said he'd take care of that. When he said he wanted to meet us at a place where his son spent a lot of time, I immediately thought of Heidegger's Cat. I blurted that out before I stopped to think. He said he would meet us there the next morning at nine.

The bar was in the ghetto just beyond the university. I'd only been there at night when it served cheap beer, burgers and fries. It was a popular place, especially with white students who got a kick out of venturing into dangerous territory. I'd heard rumors that during the day the menu included drugs, sex and guns. In the daylight the decaying bar and surrounding neighborhood looked like a war zone. Considering that the Brims and the Rolling 50s both wanted this turf, I suppose it was. My battered Chevy blended in with the cars in the neighborhood.

I saw Tweener sitting at a sloping table, talking on a cell phone. He switched it off and put it on the table when I joined him. Tweener was a tall, lean young man with lighter skin than mine. As a sophomore and a junior, Mike Morris started for the basketball team as an undersized power forward. He made up for his lack of size with determination, timing and smarts. In his senior year he was replaced in the starting lineup by a taller, stronger player. He made several attempts at professional basketball in the United States and Europe but found that he was too short and not explosive enough to be a forward. His quickness and outside shooting didn't reach the incredible levels required of a pro guard. Stuck in a body between what was needed for either position, he became known as Tweener.

Tweener gave me a hard look. "Man, this is one bad idea."

"Then why are you here?" I asked.

He shook his head. "Staying away would be even worse. What do you know about this dude, Robert?"

"Mr. Adeleye? He's on the staff of the Nigerian embassy, a secretary or attaché or something like that."

Tweener glared at me. "Chucky said his dad was head of security."

"Okay. He's head of security. What difference does that make?"

"Man, do you ever get that head of yours out of your books? The man knows about weapons and interrogation, probably about torture, too. He's going to ask us about Chucky. What we have to do is keep our cool. Be respectful and tell him nothing."

"There's not much I can tell him," I said.

"That's it. Stick to that, Robert."

A group of ebony-skinned men wearing mirrored sunglasses pushed through the door. Two by two they walked through the bar, looking into every corner and inspecting every customer. Two of them stopped by our table and stood without speaking. The other customers were hustled out and told to stay away. Two of the men took the barkeeper through an open door into the kitchen and closed the door behind them. I suspected that there were other men outside surrounding the building.

One of the men standing by our table pulled out a cell phone and spoke into it in a language I didn't understand. Then Adeleye entered. He was a massive, heavily-muscled man. His skin was so black that it seemed to have a blue tint to it. His tailored suit cost more than the combined value of everything I owned.

He spoke in a deep, angry voice: "Gentlemen, thank you for coming."

I said, "I'm very sorry for your loss, sir."

Adeleye stared at me. "Can you even imagine what the death of my son is like for me?"

"No, sir, I cannot."

Adeleye turned toward Tweener. "Can you?"

Tweener shook his head and looked down.

"At least you do not pretend," Adeleye said. "That is something. Not much, but something. Charles was the one son I had who might have been able to step into my shoes some day. The others are either mindless thugs or too soft to survive. He was my only hope that our family would be able to thrive in the world community that Nigeria is finally entering. Now my hopes are dead."

He sat down at the table.

"I am both a man of the modern world and a man of tradition. In my traditional culture, when a young man of promise dies, we hold an inquiry into why he died. People accused of contributing to his death are given a chance to prove their innocence. That is why you are here. Robert, you were his roommate. Tweener, you were his friend. I ask you, why did he die? I know he overdosed on heroin. That caused his death. My question is, why did you allow him to die?"

"Is this a trial?" I asked.

Adeleye glared at me. "The trial may come later. We will follow the customs of my country here. If it comes to a trial, it will not be like any trial you have ever seen. I understand that in English one meaning for the word trial is ordeal. That is what you might face."

Tweener said, "You can't do this. You could get in big trouble."

Adeleye shook his head. "I can do it. I have diplomatic immunity. My men are embassy staff. Speak to me or I will draw my own conclusions. Then it will go hard for you. Robert, how did you help my son Charles?"

"I tried to be a friend to your son. At first he was interested in classes and studying. Then he started hanging out with a fast crowd all night, sleeping through classes and not doing assignments. When I found out he was using drugs, I warned him. I warned you, too."

Adeleye looked at Tweener. "Tweener, besides supplying him with drugs, how did you help Charles?"

Tweener sneered at me and said, "I don't know what Robert told you about me but keep in mind that he's what we call an Oreo. He's black on the outside, but inside he's lily-white. Chucky got bored with studying all the time. He wanted to be a playa'. I introduced him to some tight girls and straight brothers. Maybe I shared some weed with him once or twice. I never touched coke, meth or heroin with him. Chucky got into that on his own."

144

Heidegger's Cat

Adeleye asked me, "What do you say about that?"

I answered, "I don't know. I stay away from that crowd. I've got to keep my grades up to keep my scholarship or I go back to the hood. I want to qualify for funding for med school later on. Tweener tried to play his way out of the hood. He made it. I'm trying to study my way out."

I paused. "I do agree with him in one way: Charles decided to take drugs on his own. Nobody forced them on him. He caused his own death."

Adeleye glowered at both of us. "Charles paid for his mistakes with his life. He has been punished. But there are others who share the blame and they must be punished, too. You offer nothing but excuses. I am not surprised. You are like your ancestors — weak. They were slaves in Africa because they were weak. That's why my ancestors sold your ancestors to white men to be their slaves here. Robert, you let Charles down. Tweener, you introduced him to the people who sold him drugs. That's why I hold you both responsible for Charles's death."

"We didn't give him drugs," Tweener insisted. "Other people are guilty of that."

Adeleye said, "I know. I will find them, too. I will find everyone involved in my son's death. The guilty will be punished. I promise that. I will start with the two of you."

He reached into his suit coat. Tweener flinched. I blinked. Adeleye brought out his closed fist. When he opened his fist, half a dozen dark brown, kidney-shaped beans fell on the table.

"Calabar beans. They come from the doomsday plant. We call them esere peas. In my country a man accused of murder can prove he is innocent the way our ancestors did. He can publicly swallow one or two beans. If he lives, that demonstrates his innocence beyond any question. I once saw four men divide a bean to decide which one of them would end up with a worthless woman. They all died in agony. The woman left with another man who later wished he had died, too."

I stared at the beans on the table.

"You can each swallow a bean or I can have my men force one into your mouths and hold your jaws shut. It does not matter to me which way you take them."

Tweener shoved the table at Adeleye and jumped to his feet. Adeleye's men tripped him, drove him to the ground and wrenched him over and onto his back. Two men knelt on his arms. While two others immobilized his legs, a fifth man pinched Tweener's nostrils closed. When Tweener opened his mouth to breathe, the man dropped a bean into it.

"If you spit it out, I will have you killed very slowly, very painfully. Three of my men used to work for Idi Amin."

Tweener started to cry, keeping his mouth closed.

Adeleye looked at me. I picked up a bean, took a breath, put the bean into my mouth and swallowed it immediately. The taste was as bitter as sin. Almost immediately my mouth filled with saliva. I began to gag. My heart pounded. My face got hot. I stood up and ran to the bathroom. On the squalid floor in front of a toilet, I knelt with my sides heaving and tears streaming down my face. Finally I vomited the entire contents of my stomach. I thought I would die right there with the smell of human excrement in my nostrils, but slowly my heaving lessened. I don't know how long I stayed on the grimy floor, happy just to be alive.

I had to think. I had never heard of calabar beans but I thought about their effects. They had to contain toxic alkaloids. I had not chewed the bean. Vomiting got it out of my system. That was consistent with its use as an ordeal. Some who undergo the test live; others die. There was a harsh traditional African wisdom to the process. An innocent person, wishing to prove innocence, would swallow and purge. A guilty person, fearing to show guilt, would hesitate and then have trouble swallowing with a dry mouth. The longer the bean remained inside the body, the more toxins would be released.

Adeleye had plans to track down the pushers who had sold drugs to Charles. He wanted to add African killings to the home-grown drive-bys and our slow self-inflicted genocide through drugs and violence. I ached for Adeleye's loss, and I myself had fantasized about cleaning out the "business" men and women whose drugs and lifestyles poison young Blacks. But I knew "collateral damage" from the conflict would import new horrors to the community already drenched in violence and despair.

When I could, I stood up. Gingerly I walked out of the bathroom and back into the bar.

Tweener was dying near the front door. From his contorted position, I knew he was out of his mind, feeling pain beyond misery. I didn't like the man. He'd been quick to taunt and belittle me. He bought into the sports delusion that destroys so many young black men. He thought sports would make him a million-aire and a star, that he'd be set for life after a few years in the pros. When that didn't happen, he settled for being a minor celebrity and a pusher of lightweight drugs. On the other hand, he was smart and persistent. He had hung on until he earned a university degree. Once the sports fantasy finally died, he might have wised up and made something of his life. He deserved a chance, anyway. I felt anger start to build within me about an-other brother's wasted life.

Adeleye and his men sat around tables and watched Tweener's life drain away. They nodded to me and I joined them.

I did not think Tweener should die surrounded only by strangers.

I remembered. In the fourth grade the word came down to me. Only girls study hard. Don't be too white. If I'd had Tweener's physical skills, I might have looked to sports to earn respect. I might have become one more body in the pipeline of young brothers served up in sports arenas as gladiators to entertain the man. Most sports encourage brothers to maim and cripple each other while the crowd cheers them on. I didn't have those skills so I endured the taunts, name-calling and occasional ass whippings but I studied hard. I graduated valedictorian, which led to more scorn.

My low SAT scores puzzled me until I actually got to college. Then I found out how badly educated I really was. My most advanced high school classes did not mention Christopher Marlowe or quantum physics. I had to have tutors and audit the hard classes before taking them for credit. My first-year grades were so low that I nearly lost my scholarship. I knew that if I failed, it would confirm other students' prejudices about my entire race. I survived, like I survived in Heidegger's Cat. And I learned one thing that the Asian kids seem to know at birth: I may not have the background to compete or the highest intelligence, but I can outwork and outstudy any son of a bitch on the planet.

Almost as if he could hear me thinking about him, Adeleye said, "I did not expect to see you again. According to our traditions, you have been tested and found innocent."

He still sounded angry.

"Thank you," I said.

I looked at the men sitting around and began to speak. "Let me talk to all of you. Mr. Adeleye accused me of complicity in his son's death due to my failure to look out for Charles. I was tested and found innocent. Now I make the same accusation. I ask for the same trial."

I looked at Adeleye.

"One man deserted your son in an unfamiliar culture that kills young black men every day without regret. When notified of difficulties, that man said he was too busy to respond. He did nothing and Charles died. Of all the people in the world, that man had the greatest capacity to help. He did nothing except blame others for his failure to act."

I paused.

"He did nothing to save his own son." I focused my eyes on Adeleye. "I accuse you."

Adeleye shook his head. I picked up a stray calabar bean from the table.

"You say you are a man of tradition. You say that in your culture when two men disagree they may duel to see which one is lying and which is telling the truth."

I took out my pocketknife and cut the bean in half. I picked up one half, put it in my mouth and swallowed it.

"I say you are responsible."

Adeleye shook his head again. "Don't think you can come in here like one of your American cowboys and challenge me to a gunfight. You have no rights here. You cannot tell me what to do."

When I headed toward the bathroom, Adeleye was staring at the piece of calabar bean in front of him and sweating. The men were staring at him and leaning toward him. Half an hour later, hunched over in pain and holding my sides, I staggered out of the bathroom. The place was as empty as a tomb.

A few days later a friend and I were reading different sections of the paper in the student union when he let out a whistle.

"Listen to this," he said. "You remember that they found

Murder Manhattan Style

Tweener's body lying on the sidewalk. They suspected he died from a drug overdose. Well, they did an autopsy and determined that he died from alkaloid poisoning. They're not sure if he died by accident, suicide or murder. How strange."

"At least they can't say we're all junkies," I said.

"You're finally sounding and looking like your old self," said my friend. "Even you can overdo studying, you know. For a while I thought you had mono. Did you find anything interesting in your section of the paper?"

"I see here that the Nigerian ambassador has appointed a new head of embassy security," I said.

"Is that interesting?" my friend asked.

"It is to me."

Author's note: This was included in Medium of Murder, *Red Coyote Press (2008). The anthology was a finalist in the Fiction and Literature category of the National Best Books 2008 Awards. I want to thank Susan Budavari and Suzanne Flaig for their editorial help with my story.*

A Lady of Quality

Listen here. I grew from a child to a young woman in the time between the murder of Emmett Till for whistling at a white woman and the murder of Medgar Evers for advocating equal rights for us. Just so you know, that was from the middle 1950s to the middle 1960s. Of course, there were other murders in Mississippi during that time. Reverend George Lee and World War II veteran Vernon Dahmer were slain for their ungodly, un-American belief that, finally having the right to vote, we should actually register and vote.

I remember being confused and scared, which was, I suppose, what the white people in power wanted us to feel. I was too young to vote. I was just trying to earn my keep in Martinville when I heard that Mrs. Wallace Morton Edwards IV was looking for a part-time maid. Her housekeeper, Eppie May Washington, was getting on in years. She needed help with the heavy cleaning and serving meals when Dr. and Mrs. Edwards had company. More than a few women had been hired, but Mrs. Edwards did not keep any of them for long.

I was strong. I'd chopped cotton and worked in the fields, trading my sweat for small wages. Every once in a while northern tourists would pull their cars over to the side of the road and take pictures of us, like we were animals in the zoo. Although I was proud of being able to do as much work as any

151

man, the ache in my back, shoulders and arms reminded me that stoop labor would eventually leave me with crippling pain. I didn't know then what another kind of work would cost me.

In the years before doing field work, I'd hauled water, cooked, cleaned and looked after the children for Ray and Eva Hooper who boarded me. You see, my parents died when I was two and my sister was an arm baby. A kind man, William Dupree, who was not kin, took us in. He and his wife cared for us until I was ten and my sister was eight. Then he passed. On his deathbed, he made Mrs. Dupree promise to keep us together. Let me tell you, she didn't. She farmed us out before his body got cold. I went to serve one family, and my sister served another. Neither side of my family and none of the good members of the church objected or offered to keep us. I did well in the rickety, dusty school where coloreds could go, but nobody noticed except my teachers. Nobody noticed anything I did. They only noticed when my chores were not done, when the children cried or meals were not ready on time. When I found that if I earned money I could keep a little for myself, I left high school without a second thought.

At that time, I had the reputation of going to church and being tidy. I thought to myself, "Maybe that's why they might give me the maid's job. Or maybe they've already gone through all the maids in town." I put on my best hand-me-down dress. I walked up to the white house on the hill. It reminded me of one of the fancy layered wedding cakes I'd seen displayed in the front window at Waterman's Bakery.

I walked past the carriage house and the magnolias to the back, to the servants' entrance, of course. First Mrs. Washington and then Mrs. Edwards inspected me like I was a fish of doubtful freshness. Mrs. Washington wrinkled her nose. Mrs. Edwards sniffed the air. Mrs. Washington was a black, sturdy woman with graying hair. Her straight nose and the copper tint to her mahogany skin showed that some of her ancestors had been Cherokees. She wore a starched apron over a dress most women I knew would have loved to wear in church. Mrs. Edwards, despite being older than Mrs. Washington, looked and moved like a schoolgirl. Her summer dress was like something out of a dream. With her pale complexion, clear blue eyes and white-blond hair, she was beautiful. She could have been my age. It set me to thinking that white years and colored years were not the same.

From the cracked piece of mirror in my bedroom, I knew what they saw. I was short, muscular and black as coal, with a nose so broad and flat you'd swear I'd been smashed in the face with a skillet.

"She's a churchgoer and not a pretty girl so she shouldn't have bucks coming to the house while she works," said Mrs. Edwards.

"She not too dirty," said Mrs. Washington.

"Not considering where she comes from," added Mrs. Edwards. "She might possibly do. It's not like there are many choices. Speak to me, child."

"Yes, Ma'am," I answered. I didn't know what to say after that.

"Do you know who I am?" Mrs. Edwards asked me.

"You're Mrs. Edwards," I said.

"That's my name. And who am I?"

I thought for a moment, not knowing how to answer. "The doctor's wife?"

"I am that and what else?"

I shook my head.

"Do you see the portraits on the wall?"

The painting closest to me showed a scowling, white-haired man with blue eyes so cold that it seemed he could freeze water just by his glare. He wore a hat shaped like a triangle pointing out at me. He wore a uniform of some sort with tight white leggings. He was not someone to trifle with. The second painting showed a man on horseback holding a naked sword. He wore a different uniform. His hat sat at an angle on his head and had long swooping feathers. His face wore the smile of a man looking to get into a tussle so he could hurt somebody. I shivered.

"Yes, Ma'am. They look scary."

"They were staunch defenders of liberty. My ancestors fought in the American Revolution and defended us from northern aggression in the War Between the States. I am a Daughter of the American Revolution and a United Daughter of the Confederacy. My great-great-grandfather Morton helped found this town. Did you know that some people say the original name of the town was Morton's Village?"

I shook my head again.

"My people are judges, army officers, congressmen and people of merit. They have been for as long as anyone can remember. I think of myself as a lady of quality with a heritage to protect and a certain image to maintain regardless of the personal or financial cost. Do you have any idea the burden that places on me?"

"No, Ma'am."

"Of course you don't. How could you? What that means, Lizzie, is that I must act in accordance with the highest expectations and uphold standards of deportment and decorum that are rapidly eroding in these troubled times. Do you understand that?"

A Lady of Quality

"Not really, Ma'am."

"Of course not. Here I am prattling away about things beyond your knowledge. Let me see if I can explain it simply.
Lizzie, I must behave properly and politely even when those
around me do not. Can you understand that?"

"Yes, Ma'am."

"If you work for me, you must do things in a certain way
because I require it. You need not understand why a thing must
be done a particular way. You need only to do it exactly as I tell
you. Do you understand that?"

"Yes, Ma'am."

"Child, you cannot know the pressure I am under. You
may look up from Colored Town and think that the doctor's wife
up in the big house on the hill has it easy. You have no idea of the
problems I face. No idea at all. Those I employ have to behave
with a certain amount of dignity because they work for me."

I nodded.

"I cannot abide stealing."

"No, Ma'am."

"I cannot allow dirtiness or sloppiness in your work."

"No, Ma'am."

"I especially shall not have a servant talk about what happens inside this house to anyone at all. I cannot have you work
for Mrs. Barker, Mrs. Scott, Mrs. White or any other of the so-
called gentry in this town while you work for me. Money, even
in large quantities, does not equate with true gentility. Obviously,
you cannot continue to work as a field hand."

I frowned, worrying about paying my bills.

She put up a hand.

"Ordinarily, I would not even dream of giving a house servant's job to a field hand, but I have heard good things about you

and you seem to know your place so I will give you a chance. I will pay a sufficient wage. For the duties you will perform, the wage can be considered generous. I will expect you on time every day without exception. When I have a luncheon or a party, I will expect you to serve. During the annual cotillion, you will assist Mrs. Washington in any way she tells you. When I do not require your services here, you can clean the doctor's office. Is that clear?"

"Yes, Ma'am."

"When I start my new girls, I give them a test," said Mrs. Edwards. "Can you set a table?"

Mrs. Washington, standing behind her, gave her head a tiny negative shake.

"I know how to set the table at home," I answered cautiously.

"Let's see how you do with my table." Mrs. Edwards made a graceful motion toward a polished ebony box on the table before me.

"What a pretty box," I said. "I've never seen the like."

"I should think not. Open it and set the table."

Inside the box was a set of gleaming silverware. I could tell that some were spoons and others were knives and forks but there were such a variety of shapes and sizes that I could not even imagine how many went to a setting.

I said, "They beautiful, but I don't how to set 'em out, Ma'am."

"They belonged to my great-great-grandfather Morton. This is one of very few treasures that my family has been able to hold on to. So much has been lost."

Mrs. Edwards paused and sighed.

You set them out like this, Lizzie." She laid out a place

156

setting with speed and precision. "Now you set out seven more just like mine."

I studied what Mrs. Edwards had done and carefully laid out five settings identical to hers before I noticed that Mrs. Edwards's forehead was creased and Mrs. Washington's eyebrows were raised. Take it from me, it was not a good idea for a colored woman to look too smart. It made white people nervous, which was a bad thing. I deliberately mixed up the spoons at the sixth place and switched the order of the forks at the seventh.

Mrs. Edwards's forehead smoothed out, and Mrs. Washington lowered her eyebrows.

"That was remarkably well done for a first attempt, my dear," said Mrs. Edwards. "Let me show you how to make it perfect." She corrected the sixth and seventh places. Then she moved a few utensils at other settings, as if I had made mistakes there, too.

"I'm sorry, Ma'am," I said. "I don't know why anyone would need so many forks and spoons when they only got two hands and one mouth."

Mrs. Edwards smiled. I could see her filing away in her mind another funny story about the ignorant colored maid to tell her friends. Mrs. Washington, behind her, nodded her approval.

"Nonsense, Lizzie, you did very well. You passed the test. I'm proud of you. Mrs. Washington tells me your parents died when you were very young. Is that so?"

"Yes, Ma'am, I was just a bitty child."

"Then we will be your family."

I could not imagine what it would be like to be any sort of kin to this beautiful white woman and the balding, red-faced doctor. I'd heard of the doctor. People said he accepted eggs and vegetables in payment from patients who had little money and that he did not even bill his poorest white clients. He was known to give the black doctor free medicine and supplies, claiming he'd ordered too much. The first time I went to work at the doctor's office, I overheard him say, "There's a new girl?" He rushed out of an examining room smiling, with bright eyes. He looked me over from head to foot. The light went out of his eyes. Without saying a word, he turned around and headed back toward the examining room. I remembered then that the colored maids Mrs. Edwards hired before me had all been pretty, tall, thin and light-skinned.

With time, the doctor came to treat me distantly but politely. He complimented me on the way I cleaned his office. He refused to let the secretary or the nurse give me their personal chores to do, but I don't think he ever learned my name.

Over the months, Mrs. Edwards taught me how to iron tablecloths, wash clothes and scrub floors the way she wanted. I quickly figured out that she was better at the chores than I would ever be. Once when Mrs. Edwards was away, Eppie admitted privately that Mrs. Edwards was a better cook than she was. Of course, with her social position, Mrs. Edwards hardly ever got to do what she was so good at. I learned to serve food and drink and retrieve dirty plates and glasses without attracting attention. I learned to speak only when spoken to and to remain deaf when I was spoken about like I wasn't there.

At a party more than a year after I went to work for Mrs. Edwards, Mrs. Scott drank half a pitcher of mint juleps by herself. She grabbed my arm and slurred words into my ear.

"How much is Mrs. Edwards paying you, honey? I know she's cheap and that husband of hers, with all his charity work, can barely pay to keep the roof on this mausoleum. If you come work for me, I'll pay you half again as much as she gives you.

Just tell me how much that is."

"Please, Ma'am, I gots to go to the kitchen," I said.

Mrs. Scott tightened her grip. I was trapped. I could not pull my arm away or raise my voice to a white woman. I stared at my feet and stood still.

Mrs. Edwards called out, "Lizzie, I believe we need more canapés."

"Sorry, Ma'am, I gonna get 'em."

Mrs. Scott still did not release me. I could not move.

Mrs. Edwards sailed over and, smiling, gently took Mrs. Scott's hands.

"I don't believe you've seen the garden this season," she said to Mrs. Scott. "I'm sure it's nothing to compare to yours. Still, I would like to solicit your suggestions on what might be done with it."

I fled to the kitchen as quickly as I could. Later, while I was washing dishes, Mrs. Edwards questioned me about what had happened.

"I'm sorry, Ma'am, I should have gone 'nother way to get to the kitchen."

"What did Mrs. Scott say to you?"

I told her.

"Have you been talking about us down in Colored Town?"

"No, Ma'am," I said. "Never. They don't even ax me no more."

"You don't talk about the doctor and his money?"

"No, Ma'am. 'Sides, the doctor never say nothing about money."

Mrs. Edwards nodded. "You're right, Lizzie. I'll bet the doctor doesn't even know how much money he has. He certainly doesn't pay attention to how much his charity cases cost us. You know, I believe Mrs. Scott was a little bit affected by the heat this evening. It is unusually warm for this time of year. I'm sure she was making a joke."

"Yes, Ma'am. I don't never talk about you and the doctor with nobody."

"You're a good girl, Lizzie. I'm sure you don't."

Mrs. Edwards turned to leave and then turned around to face me with a smile on her lips. Her eyes were ice cold.

"I'm concerned, Lizzie. In this heat, people need more liquid than usual and Mrs. Scott appeared dehydrated this evening. The next time we have her over, I want you to make sure to offer her a fresh libation every time her glass is empty. Can you pay particular attention to that, child?"

"Yes, Ma'am."

After Mrs. Edwards left the kitchen, through the closed door I could hear her talking to the doctor.

"My stars, sugar. I swear Mrs. Scott's liver must be as pickled as a beet. With all the alcohol in her body, if she died, they couldn't cremate her for fear of setting the entire county on fire. Can't you recommend a nice health spa to her husband where she can dry out? Tell me. Was she really on a European trip last year, or was she in a hospital for her drinking?"

Eating dinner the next day with just Eppie in the kitchen – Mrs. Edwards was at a church meeting – I repeated the conversation for her. She cut loose.

"You gots to be careful, Lizzie. White folks ain't like us. Wasn't smart to say exactly what Mrs. Scott say. Now Mrs. Edwards know you can repeat 'xactly what she say, too. It's better not to show what you can do."

I noticed tears in her eyes as she continued, "You might think that working for they family, givin' the best years in your life they wouldn't mind if you needed an extra hunk of ham when you have family with hungry babies visiting. But you got to remember to ax before you pack it up because they can't abide stealing. If you forget, you got to beg to keep your job and smile grateful at 'em when they say you can't have the ham 'cause you didn't ax first and it ain't convenient."

A few months after the party, Mrs. Edwards hired a new gardener, a colored man named Charles Williams. She talked to me about him.

"Charles says he's a minister," she said. "Have you heard him preach?"

"No, Ma'am." I didn't tell her that I had gone sour on the church a while back. I had not heard anyone preach for more than a month and I didn't pay attention to what folks said about the new preacher.

"You'd think that preachers would understand how important it is to maintain standards. These days it's preachers like that terrible Martin Luther King, Jr. who embarrass Southerners on the television. They want to toss out everything we've lived by, everything that has given meaning to our lives. If this new preacher is not the talk of Colored Town, he may be all right."

She looked at me intently. I didn't say anything.

To tell you the truth, I didn't know if he was the talk of Colored Town or not. I had no truck with gossip and carrying tales. Some thought I had gotten above my place and become uppity since I started working for Mrs. Edwards. I didn't mind if that meant they left me alone.

Mrs. Edwards took my arm. I saw a kind of hunger in her eyes. I knew she wanted something from me. I had to give her something, but what?

Murder Manhattan Style

"I— I hear he fools around with the womens in the church and talks about havin' civil rights meetings."

Mrs. Edwards asked, "Will you go the civil rights meetings?"

"No, Ma'am."

Mrs. Edwards tilted her head and said softly, "It may be, Lizzie, that I need you to attend and tell me what they say. We'll talk about that later." She smiled at me. My mouth felt sour. "It's good that you told me, Lizzie."

Charles looked like a proud African prince. Lord, I'd never seen a man so beautiful. He walked around like he owned the place. When he took his shirt off because of the heat, his dark skin glistened. Once, I noticed Mrs. Edwards looking at him. She held her hands together over her breast and sighed.

Walking down the hill with me after a dinner party, Eppie told me she asked him why he worked as a gardener when his congregation would support him and he answered: "People can barely take care of their families. Whatever we do, we all labor in the same vineyard." She said he preached a lot that all people are equal in God's sight. She added, "Long as he don't try to act like we all equal, he be okay."

A few weeks later, I noticed Mrs. Edwards looking at me funny. Several times she came into the room where I was working, but she didn't say anything to me. I was tempted to ask her why she was upset, but it wasn't my place. Coloreds did not question Whites. At dinner, Mrs. Washington started to load a plate for me to take out to Charles. I noticed it was cracked just as Mrs. Edwards came into the kitchen carrying a freshly cut magnolia blossom.

I said to Mrs. Edwards, "Ma'am, this plate is cracked. What plate should we use for the gardener's dinner?"

A Lady of Quality

Mrs. Edwards stared at me as if she had never seen me before, and, for the first time, I felt afraid. She pointed to the plate that the dog ate off of.

"Use that. Don't wash it. Just put his food on it and give it to him."

I froze.

"Lizzie, you put food on that plate and take it to him. Do it now."

My insides were trembling and I thought I might faint. I scooped food onto the dog's plate, hoping she would change her mind or say it was a joke. She didn't. Mrs. Washington filled a glass with ice water and rolled up utensils in a napkin. She wouldn't look at me. With my hands shaking and tears in my eyes, I took everything out to Charles.

"Much obliged," he said.

I didn't know what would happen if I told him. Nothing good. I didn't say a word. I set everything down on a garden bench. I walked away. I stood in the shadow on the porch and thoughts came into my head. Eppie would retire soon. If I slipped into her place, I could have a better life than almost any other colored woman in town. The work wasn't hard. I wouldn't end up like many field hands, bent over and in unending pain. All I had to do was to please Mrs. Edwards and hand over my soul one slice at a time. I realized that Mrs. Edwards would never dirty her hands with spiteful acts. She didn't have to. She could dirty mine.

I walked to my room, packed my clothes in a cardboard box and took all the money I had. I walked three miles to the bus station in Petersburg. I asked the man how far north I could go with sixteen dollars. He said I could take the late bus to St. Louis and transfer to one going to Kansas City. He told me on the late

163

Murder Manhattan Style

bus I could sit anywhere I wanted. I sat in the station until the bus boarded that night. I wondered if a wounded soul could heal. I wondered what I would do the next time someone treated me like I was not there. I took a seat close to the front window. I looked ahead as the bus pulled out. I never looked back.

Author's note: This story is about a different sort of crime. It won the Best Short Story of 2006 from the Missouri Authors Guild. For this story I had the "voice" of the narrator firmly in mind as I dragged it through different critique groups and worked on my skills as a writer over a number of years to write this story.

About the Author

Warren Bull

Warren Bull is the award-winning author of more than twenty short stories as well as memoirs, essays and a novel, *Abraham Lincoln for the Defense* (PublishAmerica, 2003; Smashwords, 2010). He has published in *Strange Mysteries 2* (Whortleberry Press, 2010), *Strange Mysteries* (Whortleberry Press, 2009), *Medium of Murder* (Red Coyote Press, 2008), *Manhattan Mysteries* (KS Publishing, Inc., 2005), "Great Mystery and Suspense," "Mouth Full of Bullets," "The Back Alley," Sniplits.com, "Future Mysteries Anthology" and "Mysterical-E," among others. He is a psychologist in his day job. He comes from a functional family and is a fierce competitor at trivia games.

.